# ANGELS AND MAN

Channeled by
THE SPIRITUAL HIERARCHY
through

## NADA-YOLANDA

Published for
THE HIERARCHAL BOARD
and the
UNIVERSITY OF LIFE
by
MARK-AGE
Miami, Florida, U.S.A.

ISBN 0–912322–03–9
Library of Congress Card Catalog No. 73-90881

FIRST EDITION

Manufactured in the United States of America
by Kingsport Press, Inc., Kingsport, Tennessee

# CONTENTS

# ANGELS
# AND MAN

# MARK-AGE

## MARK AGE PERIOD

The Mark Age period is that era known in prophecies as the latter days, the harvest time, the cleansing or purification period and the War of Armageddon. It is the time promised when there will be signs in the sky or marks of the age to alert man on Earth that he is indeed in those times when there will be the ending of an age, but not of the physical world. Having begun officially on Earth in 1960, the Mark Age period is scheduled to last the approximate spiritually symbolic period of forty years, long designated in religious scriptures as the period of fasting or cleansing the old in order to prepare for the new.

Thus Mark Age is that transition period of no more than forty years, and hopefully of considerably fewer, that is ushering out the old or Piscean Age and bringing in the New or Aquarian Age, the Golden Age when man will live in love and peace in a spiritual state, both individually and collectively. Actually, the Mark Age period is the final segment of a twenty-six-thousand-year plan and program by the Hierarchal Board, which is the spiritual government of this solar system, to bring man of Earth into the fourth dimensional or spiritual state of awareness.

## MARK AGE PROGRAM

The Mark Age program is part of the spiritual or hierarchal plan and program whereby man of Earth is being informed and educated as to the meaning of this transition or Mark Age period. This has to do with his awakening to his spiritual identity, nature, heritage, powers and future, and to bringing forth on Earth a truly spiritual life and society in manners and means not even conceived as yet by most on Earth.

Man is an eternal being. Only by knowing of his true nature and potential, and of his past and future, will he be able to make the

1

necessary decisions and to take the proper steps to enable him to achieve this change-over in the easiest and most desirable manner. For these changes will occur, regardless of man's desires and actions, since the entire Earth and all on it are involved. The Mark Age program is concerned with far more than aiding man to prepare for the New Age.

Mark-Age (hyphenated) designates one of numerous focal points on Earth for the spiritual forces from higher realms which are working in the Mark Age period and program. Established on Earth in 1960, Mark-Age since then has been publishing information and education in continual periodical form pertaining to this spiritual program. *Mark Age Period And Program* contains some of the highlights from those publications, which have been read or have been heard to some degree by millions in many countries throughout the world. Although these publications have included varied types of material, most of it has been of the channeled communications through Yolanda of the Sun.

## CHANNELING BY NADA-YOLANDA

Yolanda of the Sun is the spiritual name for this time for the primary channel of the Mark Age period and program and of the Mark-Age unit. She is one of many channels or interdimensional communicators who have served man for one or more lifetimes throughout eons. There now are many such channels on Earth performing various complementary and supplementary roles within the one and only spiritual plan and program called Mark Age by many but known also under different names. Known by millions on Earth as Nada of the Karmic Board, she is a teacher of channels and is on Earth now to teach and to demonstrate man's spiritual nature and powers and to help prepare him for his own spiritual awakening and his next step in spiritual evolution.

Yolanda is a conscious channel. She does not go into trance when in communication with spiritual beings of higher evolvements. Although trance channeling is a valid form, Yolanda never has done such in this lifetime. Prior to June 1960 her channeling was through automatic writing. Since then, except for several other instances in 1960, most of it has been speaking the words aloud as she receives them through mental telepathic impression or electromagnetic beam from higher dimensions and from interdimensional and interplanetary spacecraft. Occasionally some of the communications are typewritten directly as she receives them.

With but few exceptions, the vocal communications have been

2

tape-recorded as they were delivered, then transcribed by her. Copies of many of these original tape recordings, which still remain in the Mark-Age Library of Truth, have been made for many persons since 1960. The only changes made for publication are those concerning transposition of spoken to written language. All editing has been done by Mark Age, executive director of the Mark-Age unit.

The interdimensional and interplanetary communications channeled through Yolanda and published by Mark-Age come from ascended beings in the celestial or angelic, the etheric or Christ, the higher astral or spirit, and the Earth or physical realms and from those of other planets in and beyond this solar system. Their sole purpose in delivering such communications is to help all on Earth understand and work for the spiritual awakening of man and the upliftment of Earth and everything upon it into the fourth dimension. Since 1960, initial publication and distribution usually have occurred within weeks or several months of the delivery date.

## ORIGIN OF MARK-AGE

Mark-Age is not derived from any other organization on Earth. For neither Yolanda nor Mark had been members of any group, and had not studied any channeling or ideas, having to do with the spiritual Hierarchy. Thus none of the channelings through Yolanda or the other works of Mark-Age have been influenced in any way by what others have brought forth or have conceived or have perpetuated from prior works; although much of the hierarchal information and education released through Mark-Age supplements, complements, explains, enhances or corrects that of numerous other channels and groups.

Yolanda as Nada and Mark as El Morya, in the high Self states, have worked through many others, even having helped to found some groups, but in their present Earth incarnations they have not studied such works to any appreciable extent and have not been members of, or with any influence in, those groups. Nor do they endorse and validate all of the past and current channelings and other information allegedly by or pertaining to them and other Hierarchal Board members, as released by some groups and individuals.

The name Mark-Age was revealed to Mark at Easter 1949 but no spiritual significance was given until 1955. It was not until early 1960, after meditations with Yolanda and participating in interdimensional contacts through her channeling, that the true nature and purpose of Mark-Age began to be given. Its start as a spiritual organization for Spirit's and the Hierarchal Board's purpose began with formal dedication and inauguration by Yolanda and Mark on February 21, 1960 in Miami, Florida. Since that time Mark-Age has functioned as a full-time spiritual unit of operation.


## NATURE OF MARK-AGE

Mark-Age MetaCenter, Inc. is the legal entity for works of the Mark-Age unit. Created in December 1961, it was chartered by the State of Florida on March 27, 1962 and was granted federal tax exemption as a religious organization on December 20, 1963. It is a nonsectarian, spiritual-scientific-educational society. All income prior to 1970 was through freewill or love-offering, tax-deductible contributions, which will remain one of the primary sources of support for this interdimensional, interplanetary and worldwide spiritual program. The desire and the goal are to teach and to demonstrate the Mark Age program to all on Earth, as well as to perform numerous other hierarchal plan works, for which purpose aid is welcomed from those who wish to assist and to participate.

Mark-Age is known as Unit #7 in its functioning on Earth for the Hierarchal Board. One of those functions is as coordination unit, not only between the Hierarchal Board and its Earth plane manifestation, action and workers but also for all hierarchal units on Earth. The symbol of Mark-Age is a seven in a circle. This has various spiritual significances. Specifically for Mark-Age, the seven denotes full Christ consciousness for the masses and the circle means this will be permanent or eternally closed.

Seven is the spiritual number for creation: seven rays of life or groupings of aspects and functions of God, seven Elohim in the Godhead which have created man and those of other realms, seven steps for creation, and seven bodies of man pertaining to his physical life on Earth. Mark-Age as Unit #7 also indicates it is the main focal point on Earth for Sananda and Nada, Co-Chohans of the Seventh Ray. The Mark-Age theme and motto is *Love In Action*. This is the Christ principle and function. The New Age is action with high Self, action with love.

As an externalization of the Hierarchal Board on Earth, Mark-Age has numerous purposes and functions. The primary one is to teach and to demonstrate the Second Coming of the Christ. This has two meanings: the return of Sananda, spiritual ruler of Earth, as Christ Jesus of Nazareth, and the return of man of Earth to his

4

own Christ consciousness and spiritual powers. Another major function is to implant spiritual government on Earth.

## DIVISIONS OF MARK-AGE

There are five major divisions of Mark-Age for the externalization of the Hierarchal Board upon Earth. These five, in operation and to be expanded continually, are Mark-Age Inform-Nations (MAIN), Mark-Age Meditations (MAM), University of Life, Healing Haven, and Centers of Light.

Mark-Age Inform-Nations (MAIN) disseminates the Hierarchal Board's desires, plans, news, information and expressions, via MAIN news services, informational material, periodicals, books, recordings of every nature, public appearances, and every other method of communication. It is the main route through which the Hierarchy teaches and demonstrates the educational program for the spiritual awakening and development of man on Earth, through the Mark-Age teachings, information and functions.

Mark-Age Meditations (MAM) is an interdimensional and international network of spiritual groups and individuals coordinated for helping to bring about the Second Coming and other hierarchal purposes. Established in May 1972, it originally consisted of the playing of specially prepared weekly broadcasts on tape recordings as a prelude to meditation by Mark-Age groups and members and others. Each MAM focus works on the same spiritual project during the same week, thus providing tremendous spiritual energy for manifestation of specified programs. There also are other types of MAM programs for varied interests and functions.

University of Life teaches and demonstrates spiritual living, learning, expression and growth of consciousness. Its basic structure is the twelve departments of Mark-Age. It is not a formalized system of education in any one place or manner. It does not take the place of or supersede formal educational systems or institutions, but enhances, supplements and complements them. The home, school or other environment is the classroom. There are no degrees offered. The courses, the rate of study and the benefits are determined by the Life student alone. Mastership of life is the purpose of University of Life study.

Healing Haven is the Hierarchal Board's method for presenting the best of information, techniques and research for the spiritual healing of man's four lower bodies (physical, astral, mental and emotional) and his mortal consciousness (conscious and subconscious or soul aspects). It embodies the best of past and present

5

methods for healing the whole person and explores and offers new avenues, all to aid in eliminating man's dis-ease and suffering and to help bring him into balanced spiritual expression.

Centers of Light are focuses of two or more individuals coming together for learning and expressing spiritual knowledge so as to help themselves, their fellowmen and the hierarchal program. The Centers of Light include not only Mark-Age, MAM and University of Life groups but also Mark-Age-affiliated and independent units of spiritual light workers. Mark-Age MetaCenter is the prototype of such centers, offering valuable experience and assistance.

## DEPARTMENTS OF MARK-AGE

(1) *Being:* study of the nature of Spirit, with development and use of Christ consciousness and powers by the individual. (2) *Education:* spiritual educational programs and systems. (3) *Geophysical:* study, control and development of land, sea and space. (4) *Government:* study of the spiritual, inner plane government of our solar system and how to pattern local, state, national and international governments on the same principles, ideas and experiences. (5) *Guidance:* assistance in determining courses of action for individuals, organizations and governments, based on spiritual laws. (6) *Health:* teaching eternally perfect health of mind, body and soul, and how to attain and to maintain it. (7) *Living:* increasing the enjoyment of abundant spiritual living through entertainment, recreation, fine arts and other means. (8) *Love:* instruction and demonstration in nature and use of divine love in personal relationships. (9) *Protection:* invocation of divine protection and how to secure it for one's self and others. (10) *Religion:* practical metaphysical interpretation of religions, in a nonsectarian manner. (11) *Science:* bringing forth of spiritual-scientific principles and products. (12) *Supply:* teaching and demonstrating man's ability to control material needs and products, both natural and manufactured.

# INTRODUCTION

The relationships and the responsibilities between the angelic and the man kingdoms are of great importance, yet are not understood by Earthman. Instead of divine truths, man here has been plied with man-made conceptions, descriptions, definitions and fallacies through writings and paintings. The purpose of this book is to present a true revelation of this subject.

In addition to presenting the actual nature of the angelic forces, and their relationships and responsibilities to and for man and other kingdoms, it reveals facts not known by those on Earth in recent times, and also corrects many misconceptions.

The eleven discourses are the actual words of the seven archangels as channeled vocally through Nada-Yolanda, primary communications channel for Mark-Age, and as tape-recorded during the original transmissions. They were delivered in Los Angeles, California; a significant location, as Los Angeles means *the angels*. They were channeled from October 19 through October 28, 1971, but were not for release until permission for publication was granted in 1973.

The glossary contains explanations of one hundred and forty-five possibly unfamiliar terms. But it cannot begin to give the comprehensive information and education concerning the topics mentioned in this book, and many more pertaining to the hierarchal plan and program for the spiritual awakening and evolution of man. The basic texts and references that do provide this material are the Mark-Age texts for the University of Life: *Mark Age Period And Program, Evolution Of Man, Visitors From Other Planets, How To Do All Things*, as well as future books, and Mark-Age periodicals, including *MAIN* magazine.

Mark-Age Family members—an informal membership of those receiving Mark-Age books, publications, tapes, and who support the work in various manners and degrees—are kept informed of current hierarchal program information, education and developments. This is also available to University of Life students and others. Information can be obtained directly from Mark-Age or from the many Mark-Age Centers of Light and the Mark-Age Meditations and University of Life groups.

7

# 1. PURPOSES OF ANGELIC FORCES

## INVOLVEMENT WITH EVOLVING MAN

Michael and Maitreya record this through Nada-Yolanda for a cosmic, spiritual, triune purpose for all light workers upon the Earth at this time. Michael represents the Hierarchal Board and Maitreya represents the spiritual Sonship of God, relating to the evolution of mankind throughout this solar system, while Nada-Yolanda represents the physical-into-soul-into-spiritual consciousness on an Earth plane function. This development is absolutely necessary to understand as regards the evolutionary procedures of Spirit and Its many magnificent unfoldments for the ongoing of Its own creations throughout time, place and space.

Our purpose at this date is to record and to exemplify the angelic, celestial forces as they are involved with the race of man all through his creative unfoldment and development, all through his evolutionary, eternal space journeys in time.

There is no time, no space, no place where I am not. So speaketh the Lord God, Who is the Creative Force in eternal existence. You are in the beginning, you are through all time, you are existing unto the ends of all imaginings and procedures. In this scheme a set of explorations is presented so you may see the purpose and the inter-relationships of all creative substances, regardless of their level and purposes.

## CO-CREATION AND MANAGEMENT OF FORM

The angelic realms are created for the sole purpose of managing, directing and co-creating with God the forms that exist in and throughout all space and eternity. Wherever form exists there are angelic sources of one type or another to prepare the way; to govern in relationship to all other forms and purposes; and to prepare mankind for his entrance into that area of space, place and time, to

9

understand, to govern, to know, to expand, to experience and to move on and out of that place and sphere.

The angelic forces go before that, remain with that and stay afterward in the dissolution of that, provided it is decreed on high from the Source Itself. Since the Source is interested only in purpose, function and the pleasure of knowledge, It determines the creation and the dissolution of whatever is to be and to be experienced.

Therefore, there are levels, hierarchies and cosmic derivatives of that Source and substance Which are God or Life Force Energy. They alone are responsible for the forms, the existence and the energy manifestation of that which is immutable, eternal and magnified in multiplicities of infinite varieties. We seek your knowledge and your cooperation as regards these energy forms and patterns, and the relationship of man, who is the Son of God, to those who are of the eternal celestial realms.

## RELATIONSHIP WITH MAN

Your relationship is one of service and companionship. Your respect is one of obedience and knowledge. That is why we come as messengers of the light and bring you the incoming information, decrees and announcements where it befits your own ongoing and evolutionary processes.

In this respect we come to the present time and place of Earth where all are said to be changing, where all knowledge is to be advanced and where all respects are to be paid in proper relationship to the spiritual origin from which they have come. That is why you must understand the true nature of the angelic sources and forces that aid you and work with you and support you and give you comfort and energy in the exercises you are demanded to perform for the Hierarchy, for Spirit, for mankind as he goes from one level of creation or expression into another.

Man has seemed too long to be the only intelligent force on his planet. This is not true. All life form has intelligence, and all life form has a supervisory intelligence above it that aids and sustains it to keep that form. This is the function of the angelic forces. Some are very small and insignificant, as you would term it, in their evolutionary patterns and functions; whereas others, such as I who am Michael, are required to have the burden of an entire solar system, its forms, its creations, its balances and its interrelationships with one form of life and another.

10

# COMMUNION WITH MAN

In all of this there are gradations within the celestial comprehension and pattern. The celestial forces are not visible in any physical form throughout this solar system. They are never seen, in the sense that the form is seen, in third dimensional life, fourth, fifth, sixth, seventh or eighth dimensional frequency form on this planet, through the astral, into the etheric, and all the other planes and planets of this solar system.

However, beyond the third dimensional, starting with the fourth dimensional senses, are a rapport and a contact that clarify and make real all such communications and interrelating processes. Therefore, visions, meditations, dreams and the inner Self recognition of such forms and forces are as real beyond the third dimensional frequency form as anything you see or sense with your third dimensional, five-sensory faculties. That is why those on astral, etheric and planetary grades can commune, and accept Hierarchal Board manifestations and subsequent communications, with those who represent the celestial forces throughout this universe.

I am not so concerned with what you know and experience beyond the third dimensional at this time as I am concerned with what you will come to know, will come to accept and will begin to accept here and now while you still remain in the third dimensional frequency form and prepare for your fourth dimensional comprehension and consciousness.

# SUPERVISION OF THOUGHT PATTERNS

Celestial energies are created in order to sustain life form derived from thought patterns. That is why they are not apparent, nor seen, in any of the other dimensional frequencies any clearer or more definite than they are on the third dimensional. For thought is a thing. Thought collects and congregates and amplifies itself. It can create new thoughts and substances within that thought realm.

Therefore, it is the process of angelic sources to keep congregations of thoughts in those areas wherever they might be concerned. If it is a tree form, for example, it has a source of managership above and beyond that particular creation. The whole realm of trees, let us say the whole species, is governed and managed and kept in a frequency form via the angelic sources that supervise it and keep it in a structural managership in balance with all other sources and forms to which it relates and with which it interpenetrates.

11

Every single tree, therefore, has some aspect of this governing or superimposing over it. These are the devic and elemental kingdom relationships to those of the celestial and angelic realms above and beyond, generating the genesis of tree life or tree formation. So it is with every species, with every form.

The general pattern has its angelic governor or partner who keeps it in absolute communication and balance with its purpose and function and its interrelationships with every other form or genus, while the individual or specific form within that species has a devic and elemental creative aspect who is responsible.

## SUPERVISION OF MAN'S THOUGHT FORMS

As we have indicated, thoughts of men are formed, and require a certain amount of control and supervision beyond, what man has come to recognize on this third dimensional plane so far. He would not require this had he the awareness of and the operation of his full Christ or cosmic Self in and through the third dimensional frequency.

When man fell into matter and became only physical matter and lost his connection consciously with his superconscious or spiritual Self, he was assigned a great many angelic forces who would take the place of and substitute for that function which is man's own function for himself in the realm of thought.

For thoughts become forms. Those forms then jell and take on substance, energy and creation of themselves. This is the reason you have so much negativity, upset and error on the Earth at the present time, as you have created thought forms which of themselves seem to generate an energy and a pattern that you wish were not there and could be dissolved. But they cannot be dissolved until equal and stronger thought forms nullify and counteract that which you as mankind have created upon the Earth planet at this time.

Above and beyond all these thought forms are substances or agents of the angelic realm who have supervised loosely these thought forms and these energy manifestations, regardless of whether they take on a third dimensional frequency form or not. In other words, if enough men have created a thought and have given it substance and energy by their emotions, although it does not take a form such as a building or a movement or a belief or a person, a personification of that thought form, nevertheless it exists and is supervised or kept crystallized in energy expression by angelic sources or forms who are responsible to that energy that

12

has been created, has been developed and has been enhanced or has been enforced by desire, love, hate, emotion in general.

In order to reach these thought forms you likewise must reach the governorship or the imperfect development of these ideas, regardless of whether or not they are held there by a positive or a negative polarity of substance. Angelic forces, in this sense of negative and positive polarity, do not have preferences, ideas, generalities of their own. They merely are assigned, and find themselves in the position, to coagulate these thought forms and to keep them from spilling over into other areas that would not welcome their energy form or their interference or their broadcasting elements.

## CONTROL OF THOUGHT FORMS

Let us recognize that all thought, being a thing, has within it form and substance, or the elements. Regardless of whether you see those elements and can manipulate them physically or not, they are the elements of which cosmic energy is made. Therefore, the angelic forces are your best guardians and friends, in that they keep them controlled and circumscribed where they belong so they do not broadcast out or do not energize any other thought or form which would block up or interfere with the ongoing spiritual energies and expressions which the negative ones would seek to destroy or to circumvent.

This is part of divine law, divine creation, divine wisdom. You may not understand it, you may not believe in it, you may not like it, but that is of no consequence to Divine Mind. For It exists, It works and It has Its reasons of Its own, which are impersonal and perfect, in Its own workings-out of cosmic law and divine evolution.

So, you see that that which you think is broadcast and becomes a thing in substance and energy because it interferes with, it enhances or it neutralizes another series of thoughts, energies and patterns coming from elsewhere.

## INSTRUCTION ABOUT MAN'S BODIES

If you recognize all of this, can see the subsequent reasoning and consequences of this energy and source of your own being, which is thought itself, you then become much more responsible, much more selective, much more determined in what you do, think and develop in yourselves as spiritual sons of the ever-living and ever-loving God in creation.

13

That is why we instruct and expect that you will become perfected in these thinking patterns and developments, that you then will band together and will link one with the other so your thoughts become as one united thought for good and can overcome and destroy, in the happier sense, that which is of a nonproductive, nonusable, nonpurposeful function.

Man is not yet at the point where he can supervise even his own body structure on the physical. He is equipped even less on the third dimensional frequency or Earth planet to supervise his own light-body structure, as it represents the God Self within him and expresses outwardly, touching all other life form and influencing all other light form.

It is true the physical structure itself touches all other life form. But the light body, which is the vehicle through which the spiritual aspects and powers and talents and knowledge of God express, touches the invisible worlds and the other creative forces such as the elemental, devic and angelic sources or creations of the Godhead Himself.

Therefore, since man is not equipped yet to understand even his physical structure and form, and is so much less equipped on the physical, third dimensional Earth plane to handle his light body at this point in evolution, we must continue to guard, and to act as guardians for, this development, this expression and this experimentation as he does progress and evolve from that third dimensional frequency form or Earth body into his fourth dimensional aspect.

You know, of course, that you have an astral body which is a way station or in-between area of expression before you are released into the etheric body or the light-body manifestation. That too must come under control and conscious application during this progress or progressive period of time, going from third into fourth dimensional frequency form, as far as the entire planet and all life upon the planet are concerned.

## RELEASE BY MAN NECESSARY

Therefore, we ask your indulgence when we give you these specific and intentional natures of creation, and seek your natural cooperation and understanding so you can come into your natural handling and control of them as we go on and teach, demonstrate and release to you those supervisory qualities, purposes and functions that are yours to behold and yours to take hold of. We seek this more than you can possibly know. For our functions, our

14

needs and our attentions are required elsewhere. We wish to be released to our natural functions and our higher goals and purposes throughout all creation as well as you do.

It is not to be seen for many eons of time that our relationships can be released. But always will we have some cooperation and corresponding purpose. Always will we go before you in creative substance and energy to hold forth the form and the energy patterns as thought out from the Godhead or the Creative Substance Itself. Always will we be responsible for manifesting or coalescing these thought forms into some substance, energy formulation, that you can step into as the race of man and see and know and taste and experience as a governor of source, energy, form, to become more proficient in your co-creatorship with God.

God is source, substance, energy and form in all ways. You, as well as I and all angelic source, being part of that Creative Force and Source, can know and can experience our various faculties and functions within that specialization for which we were and are created to be. In this is the pleasure of ongoing, in this is the expansion of consciousness. In this is the experience for those sources and forms which follow in evolutionary procedures, too.

## TRIUNE PURPOSE OF ALL LIFE

For none are as they were, none are to remain as they are. And none are to know the final or lasting or end steps of the purpose of their creation, for there is no such thing. In the refinement of every form, of every source of Creative Energy life, a triune purpose exists: to be, to know and to act.

As this is the fundamental principle of Life Force Itself, then no form you recognize, be it a stone or a man or an angel, can ever end his being, knowing and acting out. Regardless of what is thought by you now, it is possible to think beyond, to know beyond and to act beyond that which you have at your command and as part of your resources in the present time.

## GUARDING OF THOUGHTS AND FORMS

You know only the four elements of the Earth. And you suspect the elemental energy sources and forms beyond this third dimensional frequency planet. You can hardly guess, seriously speaking, of what is high and above and beyond anything introduced by us to your conscious mind right now in the way of new discoveries, new realizations, and even those imagined energy forms comprising those elemental creative principles.

That is why we have our purpose and function as angelic forces. We have to take these forms and thoughts and hold them. Otherwise, they would run rampant and intermingle with those which already are in operation elsewhere. For if they were to interfere with what now exists and what is in the formation stages of what is possible, we could not have continuous expansions regarding evolutionary unfoldments of this energy force, beyond time and space, in the places you know not of, in the areas you cannot comprehend at the present.

It could nullify and destroy everything in the aborning stage. Just as man often destroys his best thoughts and best intentions by taking them out and examining them and rationalizing over them constantly, arguing and disrobing and probing their interiors as they come into his conscious mind from the subconscious and superconscious memory patterns, so he would be doing the same throughout eternity if I and the forces of light through the angelic realms were not protecting and not guarding against such probings and destructive tendencies.

## LIGHT BODY OF MAN

This will be controlled, of course, as man goes into his fourth dimensional, spiritual consciousness and light-body faculties. This is only the negative or peculiar aspect of third dimensional or mortal experience as he knows it in this level of his evolutionary growth and graduation.

But beyond that stage, when in the light-body form, in the Christ consciousness of that light-body form, he is not subjected to that intellectualizing, rationalized and destructive tendency. At least he is not subjected to it to the degree that he is in the mortal and negative vibration of Earth, and it does not have the same effect upon his ongoing evolutionary expression in that form and frequency.

That there are those who are beyond this stage of evolutionary grace is well known and well accepted. You have them in communication. You have them in meditation. You have them in your ongoing and evolutionary periods beyond the Earth planet. They are within your subconscious and superconscious memory patterns.

For let us remind you of one thing here. Man is not confined only to the Earth plane evolution, karma, and reincarnation cycle. He has, between incarnations of the Earth plane function, a great

16

many experiences which build into his subconscious memory pattern, as a soul through the astral body, a number of spiritual or light-body experiences of the superconscious spiritual Self that encourage him and do not release him from that at any time.

So, no matter how far off he goes from his spiritual track and his spiritual goal and function as a Christed being, he still has a certain amount of connection with it, either through the superconscious memory pattern or the subconscious, astral, soul connection of past incarnations or inner plane experiences before life on Earth and between the various lives he may experience on Earth or in other planets or places throughout the solar system.

## GUARDIAN ANGELS

That is why he never can be without this guidance and guardianship. That is why he has within himself and for himself, attracted to himself and adhered to himself, that angelic guardian who is his own special thought form. That is one of the things that must be known and accepted at this particular time for man in order for him to evolve beyond the grace and graduation period of this third dimensional frequency form as he prepares for his light-body frequency form.

Our guardian angel, first of all as far as man is concerned, is his own Christ Self. But over and beyond that is an angelic force, substance, energy creation, an individualization from out of the celestial planes who guards and guides that light-body form which houses the Christ or cosmic consciousness that is in man at all times.

Man is part of creation or God. He therefore has cosmic or God Self consciousness within his being as the seed and the purpose of his present form, his present personality, and all the problems he has carried into this life from past lives, past experiences and future functions that are his alone to perform as an individualization of that God Self or Creative Energy Force.

## GUARDING MAN'S LIGHT BODY

Guarding this evolutionary process of his spiritual Self or God consciousness is the angelic or celestial force who keeps intact the light body which is the form, vehicle, expression of that God seed within. It is not within man to have the light body, but it is being formed and developed by his greater expansion of his God Self within his own conscious consciousness or awareness.

17

As much as he will let it, as much as he will explore it, as much as he will credit it with the source and the purpose of his own being, that is as much as that God Self seed within him takes root, expands, grows, nurtures, and brings fruit into his own being. This encourages or allows the light body to form, to develop, to grow and to take anchor over and through and beyond and superseding the energy structure which you call the third dimensional frequency form or physical body.

That which you think is your home and your place and your total being is but a house or a vehicle through which you express consciously upon the Earth at this time, utilizing those elements or energies that are corresponding to the particular planet and its needs and its interrelating functions with all other life form upon that third dimensional planet which you call the Earth, the four elements we mentioned: light, air, water, and soil or the mineral kingdom.

But beyond this is the light form, which has correspondingly in common the one denominating factor that exists throughout all time, place and space: that energy force called light. However, in addition to light are other elements and forms from those elements which you do not recognize and cannot control from the Earth plane consciousness or from the Earth plane elements as you understand them.

These have supervisory elementals and devic principles that govern the form, and angelic identities which keep it in proper juxtaposition and conscious rapport and relationship with all other elements, forms and purposes regarding its evolution and place in the scheme of Hierarchal Board developments for that planet, that solar system and that galaxy or universe in which you are involved and through which you are evolving.


## USE OF LIGHT BODY

Therefore, those who see and know of a guardian angel—beyond the nomenclature and consciousness, let us say, of a spiritual Self identity and purpose—are not incorrect in assuming there is such guardianship over their form and substance. But they may not be in contact with it. Others are. If you are in contact with the angelic creative source and substance of your own body and form, then you can converse with it and can receive from it many helpful and gradual uplifting collaborations.

Until you come into the full Christ consciousness and powers upon the Earth, you will need and will require this supervisory

18

personage or identity to keep the form intact and anchored where it is supposed to be. By corresponding with it—communicating, if you will, with this intelligent force and the higher elements, as you do not understand and cannot describe them—you can learn gradually how to govern and to use and to work with this supervisory experience of your own light body in anchoring through the physical rapport or essential matter.

Since you must live on the Earth, since you must exist in the elements of the three-dimensional frequency sphere of the planet as you now know it, then you must correspond to it, as well as to the higher faculties and functions beyond it, in order to sustain a form or a physical energy pattern until the light body is equipped, ready, and finds it necessary, to absorb completely that energy impulse, superseding it and acting for it.

But since we already have said that the light-body elements are not of the four elements of Earth, with the exception of the one common denominating element of light, then you must recognize the fact that you need the operation of both elemental bodies simultaneously until you no longer require or need to express physically for this planet's structure and services.

## INFLUENCES FROM OTHER PLANES

Let us clarify that also. You may live on the Earth, through the Earth and influence the Earth plane matters without a physical body. This is being done all the time by many astral forces. First of all, some of them should not be influencing the Earth, for the good of the Earth. And many of them are influencing the Earth because they still are attached, attracted and important to the Earth sphere evolution and to the karma that has been incurred through their past incarnations and influences.

But also, in addition to that—as you well know and because we have seen fit to give you the instruction of Hierarchal Board influences, etheric masters and the light bodies of those who do influence the spiritual consciousness, the spiritual missions of mankind on Earth—you know we have the light-body structures of the ascended masters who have gone beyond any astral influences, needs and karma evaluations to be on, to be within, to supervise those Earth plane matters; although their light bodies are not seen, not felt, only implied or sensed through the fourth dimensional consciousness and the supersensory Christ powers and talents of those who are selected to see and to know these things for the ongoing evolutionary purposes of mankind as he struggles from out of third dimensional frequency form into his fourth dimensional spiritual consciousness, powers and life expression.

## LIGHT BODY TO SUPERSEDE PHYSICAL

You now are at that point where you are about to bear witness to the light body as it supersedes the physical structure, as it plays a part in the physical matter of Earth and destroys the lesser thought patterns, energies and less-than-good purposes. For this was it created. For this will it live eternally. For it is the eternal seed or consciousness of God Himself in you as an individualization of this immutable, eternal and ever-diversified God Source and Force throughout eternity and evolutionary graduations.

Man as you know him on Earth is but a temporary shell or house, to experience, to know, to be in contact with other elements, other forms, other areas of exploration of this God contact or Source of being. You have no more responsibility to the lesser forces, and only should have full and total comprehension and dedication to those sources that are beyond the physical, mortal experiences, expressions, explorations and deeds.

But this takes time and this takes deliberate planning and a great deal of discipline by you as you now express in the mortal flesh. In order to circumvent and to supersede that energy level and to grow beyond that elemental expression of your body and consciousness in a third dimensional form, you must now come into contact with the devic elements that control all other light force and form on which you are dependent for physical life, then graduate to the angelic force which holds those thought forms in place, so they can be dissolved gradually, uniformly and without disturbance to the Earth pattern as you now know it.

For if you do not do this peacefully, gradually, lovingly and in the highest consciousness of all, destroying what already exists upsets the entire balance of the interrelating forces as you now have them in expression upon the Earth planet and amongst the life forms that exist on the Earth planet at this time. We speak here of the mineral, vegetable and animal kingdoms, as well as your own physical form and body as you know it in a third dimensional frequency form utilizing the same four elements all the other life forms upon the Earth planet utilize and form for expression.

## ANGELIC COMMUNICATION NECESSARY

So, it is absolutely necessary for mankind, going from mortal evolutionary expression into fourth dimensional spiritual life and light, with divine love that is in him from the God Self, to communicate with those angelic forces that hold in place all these forms and life bodies as they express on the Earth, on the astral, and into the etheric and celestial realms beyond which you now are expressing in Earth and are aware of as physical forms and conscious beings, individualizations of God Himself in you.

That requirement is your next and most immediate step as sons of God, children of the light, and truth students. So be it. So, be it. So it is. For I have spoken it, and represent myself in angelic form as Lord Michael, titular head of this entire solar system and all celestial forces as they express throughout this galaxy and universe.

But also I am representing, for this time and place, Lord Maitreya, who is the Christ head and the spiritual form or mat ray for the entire Sonship of God as it expresses in this particular solar system; speaking now through the channel who is Nada-Yolanda and who represents physical form as it expresses going into astral counterpart or soul-memory pattern through the Yolanda aspects and memories while holding forth the Nada light body as it may be seen and known throughout Hierarchal Board functions for this solar system, and beyond, on the Seventh Ray. Amen. So be it in truth. It has been truth, it is truth, and truth shall supersede all error, as expressed herein. Amen.

# 2. RESPONSIBILITIES

## ANGELIC RESPONSIBILITY

Blessed are ye who work with understanding and with love. This is Uriel. Responsibility of the angelic forces is solely to the Godhead, as represented through the Elohim. We, on the other hand, have a tremendous responsibility to know and to secure the light and thought and force as they are projected from those in the areas over which we are acting as guardians.

We take from the thought projections and sustain the light form and the molecular structure as they affect the particular area, dimension, plane or planet in which we are overseeing. We must be sure that all who come into that area are able to understand what it is that their functions and responsibilities and lessons are to be. In this way our influence over each individual species is extremely long range, sometimes millions of years in the making, the sustaining and then in the dissolving and transmuting aspects.

## DEVELOPMENT OF MAN

That is why you have been given such a perspective at this time in your evolutionary development and responsibilities, also, so you can understand more fully what it is that is required of you as you go from third into fourth dimensional frequency vibratory form. It is not an overnight or sudden or short experience, but is long range and takes many hundreds and thousands of years to complete as far as an entire species is concerned.

Therefore, look not to your works and your instructions and your efforts as being something to be accomplished just once, or in the here and now only, but something you have been prepared to know and to understand, to work and to cooperate with, over a very long range of time preceding this life in other areas of instruction, planes and planets of development; this life and the ensuing ones to follow.

That is why we are so precise and careful in giving out this information, in guiding and guarding you from any hasty works and thoughts. For there is much to learn and there is much to understand and there is much to give from your level of cooperation and contact. That is why you must understand the larger scope of this procedure so you will see it in the cosmic sense and not just in your own individual planetary life; or even, in some cases, those who erroneously are thinking of just specialized or individualized functions and endeavors. It does not involve simply one ray or another. It does not involve one planet or another. It does not involve one set of workers or enlightened soul workers, as against another. For all are involved in this transmuting, lifting and changing sphere.

## SUSTAINING EARTH LIFE FORMS

There are forces over and beyond your control. That also is for you to understand, to come to reckon with, and to balance and to cooperate with. For this is extremely essential. One of these forces that are not in your command is that of the angelic realms. But we of the angelic forces are influenced by that which you as mankind project out into the ethers and is picked up by the devic, elemental forces which work with and control, balance and sustain the life form as it expresses on the Earth planet as you now know it and as you now have life sustained for yourselves upon it.

Your life force is sustained in only the physical realm and not in the spiritual or in the subconscious-astral realms. For you are not dependent upon the physical planet necessarily for these other forms, to have frequency and expression. But you are dependent upon the physical planet as a house or an avenue through which you may travel to higher expression and experience, and know that there are areas of further growth and responsibility and expression for yourselves as sons of God.

That is why it is absolutely essential that we understand this and that we work with it and sustain this planet as it now is expressing. For by destroying or eliminating the avenue through which this expression has been in existence for you as physical beings in the last twenty-six million years, we must give you an opportunity to work with it consciously, knowingly, willingly, lovingly and in a peaceful transition from one level into another.

If this were not done you would have a tremendous gap in your experience and in your normal and passive progression, which is absolutely essential. If there are tremendous gaps or areas not combined with the past, as you go into future developments it literally causes a tremendous hole in your evolutionary progress, in your understanding and in the procedures as divinely decreed and manifested from the Godhead.

## MAN'S RESPONSIBILITIES

Our responsibility, therefore, is to keep these things intact and to work with you as best you permit and as best for your own advantages that can make you responsible for those functions which are your responsibilities. These mainly are right-thinking, right-acting and right-motivation for your own existence, for the existence of the planet on which you are expressing at this time, and for all life and species that express therein.

That you do not know and do not understand consciously, in the majority sense, that your life expression expands out to other areas, dimensions, planes and planets is not what we are striving to record or to remind you of at this time in your growth and functioning. But it is sufficient for our purpose, let us say, to make you aware of what you are doing where you are. This is job enough.

Your most immediate and purposeful gains are to be realized by seeing the planet in its wholeness and in its interdependence and in its reacting functions, one area of life with another, one level of expression with another, one form of life with another. For this is how it was created, this is how it sustains itself and this is how it will be transmuted gradually and effectively with the least amount of stress and strain upon all who are involved.

## TRANSMUTATION OF EARTH

You must realize this process will take us many thousands of years to complete for the entire planet you call Earth. But mankind himself will work with this consciously and in most absorption during the next thousand years, when you will be aware of this transmuting process and the incoming light for the form we call the fourth dimensional frequency, light-body, resurrected consciousness.

This means the majority of men hovering over, working with and sustaining life on the planet Earth for the next thousand years, as you would record time, are to be consciously aware of and to work with this susceptibility to new life form in themselves and in all other creatures, as they know them.

The veils will be lifted so the energies will be seen and will be felt and will be manipulated. The consciousness will be lifted sufficiently so the majority of men will know and will understand what is coming about in their experience. Their hearts will be lifted to the point where love will predominate, cooperation will be the theme, and great desire will ensue for the expansion of this faculty and function and ability which are inherent in mankind himself.

Therefore, we who are of the angelic realms can manipulate and can re-form the light and the molecular structure so man can have this new light-body functioning or form as his predominant element. For he will see it, he will know about it, he will understand its purpose and he will desire it.

That is as far as our responsibility goes, and it is quite a major part in the entire process. But in this process, in this gradual graduation and growth of mankind upon the Earth, he will see and will know these thought patterns and these desirable purposes forthcoming. Therefore, it will be picked up by the devic and elemental forces in the planet who then can cooperate and work with him.

This is like unto and equal to the subconscious track of man within himself. In other words, if the desire and the understanding are sufficient, the projections of light and thought going from mankind as a majority on the planet can be inaugurated into the subconscious track of himself and of the planetary structure and of the life forces that sustain a form and a life upon the planet.

## SUBCONSCIOUS IN BODY CREATION

It is, after all, as you well know, the subconscious areas of your existence that create and hold the type of body out of which you are operating. The creation of the elements and the form for that body suitable for the planetary structure is the responsibility of the angelic kingdom, which is correlating to that beyond man's comprehension and responsibility as a son of God. But the devic elements are those that manipulate and create the form itself for that individualized species and individualized individuality, or personality as you might express it through the individual incarnation you express now.

In other words, you do know that it is your subconscious mind that performs the work and makes the vehicle you express in for each individual incarnation. But you cannot express a form beyond that which has been outlined and has been perfected by the angelic kingdoms for that place and that time. Therefore, a man on Earth cannot perform through a body that is alien in molecular substance

25

and structure to all the other molecular structural forms man is expressing through on that planet at that particular time for that particular series of lessons and expressions and purposes.

But the individual form he uses, the strength of that form, the weaknesses in that form, the peculiarities of that form are created or manipulated by the subconscious or the devic elements, because he already has projected, through thought, through desire and through past experience what is applicable to his own past summations of time, place, purpose and service.

The elements, of course, as you know, are peculiar unto that area of expression only. It is the elements that the devas use to make the form. Where there is a lack of certain elements in a person's structure or makeup—even astrologically speaking, in the present knowledge you are utilizing upon the planet at this time—it is because that man or that individualization has not paid or has not given homage and respect sufficiently, or perhaps has abused that particular element in his past incarnations, in his past motivations, in his past feelings about it. You therefore are seeking always to know, to understand, to work with and to appreciate each one of the elements in the area of the present expression where you are.

Light is the common denominator, for this is the life force. All the other elements, regarding this plane and planet and structure, have various purposes and needs and relationships unto your own body and structure. Where you lack in one area or another is where you lack the appreciation of and the utilization of those particular elements for their own sustaining, balancing and fruitful works.

You are not required to know and to understand all of this consciously. For in each life and in each intellectual development, as you express upon a certain area or place in the endless kingdoms of God, you have a tremendous amount of work and lessons and functioning to perform. Therefore, your subconscious mind, or the devas that are in rapport with your subconscious mind, prepare, hold, sustain and keep intact every single thought, feeling and motive you have regarding all of these ongoing experiences, functions.

## NATURE OF PLANETARY LOGOS

As you know and as we have given several times, this acts as a gigantic computer, beyond your own comprehension at this time. No one can be in total contact with this computerized effect. For it is held within the devic kingdoms, it is held within the devic responsibilities, that surround you. This is in your auric field, this is in your subconscious memory pattern and this is part of the planetary structure to which you contribute as an individual.

26

Let us take the Earth planet, for instance. Every single person who has sustained a body, a mind and a personality on the planet Earth has contributed something of some degree to the devic and elemental forces as they computerize and work with every single life form individualized and expressing throughout time as long as that planet has been in existence.

This gigantic recording device is that which makes up the planetary logos and gives it its own personality, its own functioning, its own life record and destiny. So, there is no one who is not responsible, in one form or another, to the planetary logos. The planetary logos, on the other hand, is responsible or responding unto each and every person who is upon the Earth and who ever has been upon the Earth at one time or another.

## RELATIONSHIPS IN PLANETARY LOGOS

This is another reason why it is absolutely impossible for you to think of eliminating or ignoring those who have gone on to astral forms. For they are interlocking and interconnecting with the planetary logos and with your own functioning as an individualized, personalized being with a physical form, through the thought patterns which they have projected, have implanted and have recorded on the Earth planet itself.

This interlocking, intermeshing, interchanging and interexchanging force is ever fruitful, is ever working and is never to be condemned. It may be transmuted. It may be lifted. It may be excused or forgiven, by divine love, for any errors it may have committed. And certainly it can be raised to the highest expression possible for each one of those thoughts, each one of those patterns and each one of those purposes you are striving to externalize at this time.

But you never can eliminate the procedure, the passage, of their coming and their going. For this is not possible, since you cannot destroy any life force that ever existed anywhere at any time. You merely can change it and lift it, and strive to make it good where it may have been in error.

## ATTAINING CHRIST POWERS

This understanding supersedes all other comprehensions you have been given. This understanding is absolutely essential for the full possession of the full Christ consciousness upon the Earth planet at this time. As already stated, it will take at least a thousand years for the majority of men who are going to incarnate and to be responsible for the planet as it goes on in evolution and relates to the rest of the planets in this solar system. So, you might as well begin with now for this eventual goal and purpose.

Until you have comprehended this and have worked with it you are in the learning and graduating stages of becoming that which you are destined to express upon the Earth. That is the full Christ consciousness and the utilization of the full Christ or cosmic powers throughout this planet as it affects this solar system and as this solar system works with the others in its own galaxy and universe.

May we then proceed with this educating faculty and function, and teach you how to do this so you may manipulate it and work with it and desire it to the best of your abilities where you are now. No one should feel that he must know and understand and work with this to the fullest extent that it will be possible. For he needs the cooperation of the majority of men upon the planet. That will be the function and the purpose of Sananda, who returns as Christ Jesus of Nazareth, in his next appearance upon the Earth.

## PREPARING MASSES FOR CHRISTHOOD

You who are in the advance guard of this merely are planting the vibratory rate, preparing the minds, the hearts and the desires of mankind for this knowledge and for this experimentation—or experience, as you might call it—and for the conquering of this faculty which is inherent in your ongoing process as sons of the light and manipulators of God Force or life energy.

That you will begin to do and to work and to know of this now are our best and highest hopes for man, in the minority sense. To teach and to prepare all men for this on the planet is not to be a critical consideration at this time. But after the teachings of Sananda in the next era it will be the Christ or base consideration of your higher function for eons of time. Until then, however, that is part of the angelic responsibilities as they hover over each one and each species for its own ongoing evolutionary process.

But when the time comes that you as an entire race take on this responsibility and do this work and function in the highest and most impersonal ways, from a cosmic point of view, we will go on and will leave that faculty unto you, as you are to be governors over the whole area of your own existence throughout the planetary evolutionary processes.

It is ours, therefore, to control, to guide, to instruct and to protect you and all other life forms from any mismanagement or mismanipulation of this type of functioning. But as we proceed we give a little more guidance and information and responsibility to

28

you so you can begin to flex those areas of your own consciousness and your own desires. This then broadcasts out to all others who are coming into the same level of awareness and desire, and gives them new vistas to share and to work toward.

## EXPANSION OF CONSCIOUSNESS

For man is ever a seeking and an adventurous being, stretching out beyond his confines of mortal expression, and even of soul responsibility or soul memory patterns. That which he has sought and has experienced in the past and has absorbed as knowledge is never sufficient, because the life force is inherent in him. He is part of life force. With this seed of energy and light within his being he seeks to know more of it, to express it and to expand out toward that light.

Not only is this true of man but it is true of every life or created energy form or pattern. So, never look down upon any other species, no matter how confined it may be in its expression of now, and see it not in this same energy or expanding-out consciousness, for it is so. Some take longer and have less intelligence and force and energy to drive it forth. But in your respect, that of the race of man, we see a much more conscious self-consciousness, and therefore a greater desire and ability to do these things which are part of the natural and inherent God Force Which exists within and is the primary creative functioning or fortune of existence.

We speak of many different ways in which these lessons and possibilities can come about. But there are so many complex and creative jobs to be done that we prefer not to give more than you can share comfortably with these jobs and functions as they will unfold to you gradually. But for now be receptive to the fact that there are areas beyond your control which you shall come to know and shall come to work with and shall come to learn from. This should be your most essential and primary consideration at this time. Being aware of them and desiring them and looking forward to participating in them should be the most predominant thought pattern you develop during this time.

## PLANETARY CHANGES

In speaking of the changes that come upon the Earth planet itself, therefore, you know you have a great responsibility, from the principles that have been dictated herewith; because, as you realize, the life force and the structure of the planet itself are in keeping with that of your own life force and structure as a physical being upon the planet Earth.

Since we have given you the principles and the trusts by which these structures are existing and continue to manipulate and to function, you know you have a great responsibility via what you think, how you act, and what you desire for the planet and for your own future expression as sons of God in a physical form; or in a physical form going into spiritual or resurrected form, as described by Sananda in his last incarnation as Jesus of Nazareth.

Therefore, your responsibility to the planet and the thoughts which you project out for the planetary changes that must come about peacefully are greatly severe and must be kept circumscribed to only those of the very highest motives and comprehension. We ask most seriously that those who come into the light, and recognize that they have these powers and these responsibilities and these functions for the planetary evolvement, see it as a peaceful transition of one form into another, and that never at any time see need or see desire for extreme change and severe and upsetting transmuting qualities.

For, emphasizing again, we say unto you, mankind of Earth, in the light body you can make these changes peacefully, harmoniously and controlled via the thought patterns and projections you send out; which are picked up by the devic and elemental kingdoms; who then are manipulated by us in the angelic realms according only to that which they have recorded into their computer system via your thought patterns, your thought controls, your thought desires and energies.

It is not our responsibility to do this, but yours. You are the ones that affect the devic and elemental forces as they make the change and prepare the planet for the new life form which is to come and which is to express in the many thousands and thousands of years ensuing from this age onward.

You have passed into the age of change. You have passed into the transmuting of this planet, of this life force, of your own frequency form and function as far as this planet and this solar system are concerned. The past is gone and the future is ahead. In the present, every thought, every word, every deed and every desire are going to have a great impact and importance on what is to transpire from this moment onward.

God bless you. I am with you constantly and work with you in peace and with love. For the transmuting is in the now. But the Seventh Ray function of peace and love follows according to your will, your way and your desire of expressing yourselves as the sons of light and the children of God. Amen. Uriel.

# 3. TRANSMUTATION TIME

## A NECESSARY BALANCE

Peace and love, truth and justice; Zadkiel speaking, with Uriel; archangels of the Sixth and Seventh Rays, present. It is the balance of these two functions and responsibilities that both confuse man and fulfill him in his spiritual-consciousness time. Only when this aspect of righteousness, truth, love, honor and perfect balance is achieved is man in the mortal and intellectual sense prepared and ready to step into the full Christ consciousness and thereby transmute the physical, mortal, intellectual will into the total dedication, aspects and functioning of his Christ mastership.

That reasoning faculty and perpetual confusion caused by the lower senses and the mental aspects and the soul preparation have kept the truth from being implanted, perpetrated and exercised everywhere upon this dimension for the past two hundred and six thousand years of recorded time, as you have been given the outlines of the evolution of man in this dimension.

But in the cleansing period of the Mark Age, as you have been given the nomenclature and the terminology of this latter-day period, we now can give forth the truth and the justice to make ready for love and peace. That is why I, Zadkiel of the Sixth Ray, am preparing for the Seventh Ray function of Uriel, in totally anticipating and anchoring that which is the full Christ manifestation, or cosmic man in the light body.

## SIXTH RAY OF TRANSMUTATION

The light body is pure, fulfilled and completely light, without any interference from the lower senses and the intellectual trials and tribulations of past karma, experiences, knowledge and endeavors. Therefore, it is the function of the Transmuting Ray, which is the Sixth Ray, prior to the infusion and the completion of the Seventh Ray, represented by peace and by rest from all the work that has

31

gone before, that must come prior to and take precedence over and be dominant in all activities regarding this Sixth Ray function of the cycle known as the Mark Age period and program.

So, in preparation for this time and era many have confused the issue; have intellectualized the energies and endeavors; crediting, therefore, this aspect with the highest that is to come forth upon the planet. True, it is the highest to come forth upon this planet in these end days, for it is without conclusion and without argument that the Seventh Ray faculty cannot take place, cannot be fully functioning, for the majority of mankind upon the planet until this work is completed, that of transmuting and purifying everything that exists.

So, the purple or violet transmuting activities, as controlled by and conducted and supervised in my realm, regarding atomic energy structure, is superseding that of any other force that takes place upon the planet. Yet, we ask it be done with mercy, with love and with peace. That is why you must have the cooperation, the coordination and the understanding of Seventh Ray principles involved totally and at all costs during this transmuting period of changing the area and the energies from that of violent, disagreeable, negative trial and error upon the Earth into that which is peaceful and loving and filled with cooperation and contentment.

## SEQUENCE OF EVOLUTIONARY STEPS

So, blame not totally those who have confused the times, have confused the area of responsibility and have confused the sequence of events as they must take place in themselves, in you, in the planet and in the structure regarding the elementary God-given properties to control and to house that which is known as Earth planet life in the present time and sequence of events.

Truth and justice, these are the battle cries of the Sixth Ray, in preparation for the Seventh Ray faculties of love and peace. For you cannot have one without the other. You cannot have truth and justice without knowing your purpose is for love and peace to follow. You cannot have love and peace in their own time and empirical design without truth and justice being their base of operation and their foremost forerunner for you individually and for the race of man coming and going on and through the Earth plane operation.

Truth and justice require much cleansing and purification. It is the judgment seat and it is the point in your six steps of evolution where you must separate divine law from man-made or mortal,

32

intellectual reasoning, love, desire and intuition. It sums up the five previous steps of evolution and gradual conscious expression of the spiritual man. Therefore, it is that final, culminating step in order to know the total Christ powers and consciousness.

In many cases before this empirical design occurs you have a sequence of time that rests and purifies your intentions, thoughts, feelings and knowledge. This is often why some who have endeavored to seek out the sequence of order and the sequence of responsibility or events for purification and fulfillment see the Seventh Ray aspect of love and peace fulfillment to be that in the sixth step, rather than the final, lasting and culminating step of all that takes place. It is often the mercy and the grace of the God Self within which give this as the sixth period of spiritual awakening and endeavor. You have this in many cases and in much spiritual lore.

But it is without reckoning and with no uncertain terms and total purposefulness that following that possible rest from the five previous steps—or initiations, as you might call them—you do have that most important, that most clarifying and that final step of spiritual energy before you have the total fulfillment which is the Sixth Ray activity of transmuting what was resolved and consciously received and intuitively interpreted, plus the judging of all those steps, aspects and knowledge which have been gathered during the previous uplifting and ongoing spiritual experiences.

TRANSMUTATION FLAME

No matter how much you have expressed in Christ or spiritual talents, no matter how much you have reasoned with and have reckoned your fulfillment to be, unless you go through the transmuting flames and the judgment aspect of good and error, right and wrong, positive and negative for your own individualization and your role within the entire hierarchal scheme of man's evolution as a race consciousness, you cannot step into the full endeavors, experiences and Christ talents and powers which you expect as the total cosmic Self. That is positively and finally the seventh and lasting resurrection.

It is there that all mortal, previous purposes are left behind. It is there that all responsibilities may be shed. It is there that total fulfillment is expressed. It is for this reason that Sananda has been made the chohan of the Seventh Ray. It is for this reason that peace and love must reign upon the Earth after the transmuting flame has its effect upon the Earth dimension and all life upon the

Earth dimension, including the planet, all life form and mankind himself.

It is the reason we are in the sixth step or the sixth initiation at this time. It is sometimes confused, for this reason, with the true Aquarian Age, which it is not. It is that interim period which we call the Mark Age period before the full Aquarian Age, the full fulfillment of the Seventh Ray, and the seventh step of total Christ commitment and revelation and the second resurrection, which Jesus himself shall express, shall teach and shall lead for those who are the light workers now incarnated and who will be incarnated in the next several hundred years.

You have known this in some respects. But in order to put it in explicit terms, we must take this opportunity on this level to initiate your minds and hearts to that which has your allegiance, your loyalty and your functioning. But it is not required that all know, understand or accept these principles or ideas. It is sufficient that all work toward their own purification. Under this aspect they will be feeling the Sixth Ray transmuting flame.

## CHOOSE GOOD OR EVIL

They will be dedicated in their own minds, hearts and soul endeavors to rid themselves of that which is of error and to place before their consciousness and their judgment seat of intellectual will that which is right and good for positive results and constructive realizations and to eliminate those which are less than positive and less than constructive in their ongoing as spiritual beings.

For you cannot be both. You cannot be a mortal individual and experience and express the mortal, fleshly enjoyments and thoughts and pleasures and at the same time expect to fulfill that which is of your spiritual, Christ mission. You must choose. This is where the judgment and the justice are seated, in yourself and in the cosmic realms beyond this dimension and place known as Earth.

That is why I have endeavored to use all of my energy and time to help in this selection. It is my responsibility to help in your selecting these things, by bringing them to your attention at this time as the energies are forthcoming from the angelic realms. It protects you from making erroneous judgments in yourself, in others, and regarding the Earth planet itself. Many energies or thoughts are projected out so you may see the difference between truth and error, and thus judge them.

But it is not up to us of the angelic realm to make the choice. For man has been given free will and, from his own freewill expression and his own learning growth and grace period of becoming a son of God in this era, he has that right to choose what he has had presented to him in this conscious way.

## LATTER-DAY CHOICES

So, many choices will be given in these end days and during this purification time. It should not be looked upon as an unpleasant task and a difficult one. It really should be looked upon with great pleasure. You should strive within to make it one of the most enjoyable and exciting moments of your entire spiritual experience, as far as you have come in spiritual development, because it is that moment when you utilize every power, every intuition, every intellectual, knowledgeable point and say: this will serve me in my ongoing stages and can be productive for the good of man and for my own spiritual mission and role upon the Earth and in the times to come after this mission and this life experience; or, it will not serve.

If it will not serve, then it should be without difficulty, and it should be expedient, to eliminate it. But if you choose to have both—as they say, have your cake and eat it too—you will not gain the stature, nor gain the experience, of spiritual life and spiritual good fortune. For it is impossible to have both worlds at the same time. You may live in the world and not be of it, but you cannot be of the world and be of the spiritual consciousness at the same time. This is a total impossibility.

Your choice is being made in these latter-day periods when so much is coming up before you in consciousness from which to choose. You wonder at the upheaval. You wonder at the crime and the pollution, and the many ideologies battling one another in both political and spiritual or religious fields and in the lives of man as he lives them socially.

But you know not why, or you would not be bewildered and confused. For it is all these things that have been experienced by man for the past two hundred and six thousand years of his time evolving in this dimension, cropping up into his conscious mind for that delicate choice of good or error, for his ongoing spiritual evolution. It is not the first time man has seen these things, has experienced these thoughts or has known what the results will be in the long run. It is only in this age that he can see them all consciously, concretely and concisely for really what they are, good or evil.

35

If man chooses evil at this time, after having experienced for thousands of years and many thousands of incarnations what has occurred as the result of that choice, then really and truly has he anyone or anything to blame outside of that choice that he makes? His own free will again is involved here. For he knows the truth of himself and he knows the truth of his constructive creation, which is of God, and he knows the justice of God in these things, to work out the cause and the effect of all of his choices on every single level that he may be living them: mentally, emotionally or physically.

Only by choosing the spiritual right, truth, justice, or the will of God, through his own God-given intelligence which he has been given in order to make these reasoning evaluations, can he know what is for the best in his own spiritual evolution. For if he chooses not to evolve spiritually but wishes only to evolve physically, mentally and emotionally, that choice is still his own to make. He has made that choice many times in the past.

## TRANSMUTATION OF EVERYTHING

But he still will pass through the transmuting flame or the purifying effects of this age in which he lives upon the planet Earth and in the environs known as the astral planes surrounding that planet called Earth. For I am Zadkiel of the Sixth Ray or flame of life, and produce these effects throughout all lesser dimensions, coming from the etheric down into the astral and transmuting through the Earth plane life and force. Therefore, every life frequency, every form, every thought, every desire, every experience passes through that flame in these end times.

It has been occurring, as you may have noted, for the past hundred and five years also, because in that period of time these transmuting effects have been physically obvious and effective upon the Earth planet, and have been translated from the etheric and the astral planes for the past hundred and fifty years of time.

That is why many channels, prophets or so-called mediums have been picking up all of this information in that period we record for you, as you denote time passage on the Earth in these latter days. It is that which has been predicted and has been prepared for you. So, as my processes, which I am supervising through many angelic forces, through the entire devic kingdom, and as they pass down through the elemental life which you experience as part of your daily energy and daily expression, you know that it is as a hell on fire. Much of this is what is to be interpreted as the hellfire-and-brimstone colloquialisms that were expressed in so-called biblical and other scriptural terminologies.

## TRANSMUTATION OF MAN

Man is passing through that stage at this present time, whether he be on the astral planes of life or on the physical dimension. It is quite true that many schools of thought and teachings will try to lift you above and beyond that stage. This is proper. This is right for those who have prepared themselves in advance and have worked upon this principle in many ages before this one occurred, in order to help those souls who are so attracted to that teaching or those teachers, so they can pass safely through the transmuting experiences by understanding the higher planes of activity and the etheric or Christ-consciousness aspects.

This may include many of those schools of thought you call the spiritual sciences or the mystical, metaphysical type of teachings. But it should not supersede your knowledge or your expression of service, to eliminate all others on the planet at this time who are not consciously aware of this activity and these works and cannot be part of them for their other needs, expressions and services to mankind; let us say, in other religious circles, in national or political strains, or because of educational limitations during this life span.

We speak, of course, only of this particular life span; and have reminded that all on the Earth, all on the astral have been supervised and have been aided for eons of time for this particular age. There is none who is ignorant of the inner Self knowledge about these things and the preparation for it. For you have been given this knowledge and this understanding on other planes and planets; and in prior lives, even, when you incarnated upon the Earth and studied some of these schools of thought which just now have been mentioned.

## JUDGMENT TIME

Now your time has come to transmute all that has been and was of less than truth and to bring about the justice that is the spiritual justice, the righteous judgment for all mankind as well as for yourselves individually and the life form that exists for the good of man.

You will judge each animal, each plant and each mineral in like measure as time goes on, but perhaps not in this life experience and episode. For before man will go the scroll of life and the contribution of each species so that it will be named justly by its nature of service, truth and love. In this way you refer again to your original status as purely lights on the Earth, and were given that opportunity in the beginning to name and to select that which could be part of your Garden of Eden or your paradise upon the plane where you are expressing.

But because you fell in consciousness, because you fell in service, because you mixed in so much of your own self-will and desire for power and dominion over other species and life forms, including your own fellowmen, you were conditioned to permit error procedures and less-than-good faculties to procure a foothold and to develop themselves, evolutionarily speaking, upon the planet at this time. So, you have many life forms which are undesirable to your spiritual ongoing, and even are detrimental to your physical, mental and emotional well-being, as people and children of the Son light and God Himself.

But in time you will transmute all of this and will return it unto its primal energy and will be able to give it a new life, a new nature, a new purpose and a new service in co-relation with that which you will have come to understand in that period of time when you judge and discern and select that which is good and proper for your own spiritual evolvement.

In those times will you select that which you can work with constructively and properly in all the dominions of life and all the aspects of life, and will prepare to give those over to the higher courts of judgment and selection in the areas of service which man will come to understand and to know, and which now are controlled and supervised by the elemental, devic and angelic forces through this planet, as they express now.

Anything of good will be judged to be good and spiritual. Anything evil will be given over to those forces that can learn to work with and to transmute them on a spiritual basis. For you who have destroyed, for you who have used nature in an error way, will be the ones who will have to make those decisions and to work with them in the next evolutionary period facing you, whether you are on this planet or whether you are outside of this planetary sphere known as Earth or whether you are taken far away from the entire solar system as it evolves into the next evolutionary period.

## SEPARATION OF GOOD AND EVIL

This is something you have not conditioned your minds to experience or to expect. Let us look for one single moment here to the transmuting flame or the judgment seat, as I have claimed it and have expressed it. When you separate the good from the bad it does not mean the bad is totally dissolved. It is separated from the good. It goes somewhere and performs some function and has some existence. Even though the dross is burned out of it, it still has some sediment left of its energy and its force, which still may maintain or retain memory patterns, in its subconscious function, of that which you consider error or evil.

Therefore, those who have perpetrated and have contributed to that error or evil, on its subconscious level, will be condemned or doomed with it to an existence that to them may seem eternal or everlasting, but is not, in the conditioning period of time where the two must learn to cohabit and to convince each other of their own specialities, functions and purposes in the realms where they will be discharged to, and can see how this aspect is part of a judgment and true separation of the good from the evil.

It is not recognized often that those who do choose to stay with that which is of error or ugly to themselves in the spiritual consciousness still will have to manipulate, to work with, and to condition themselves to some sort of relationship with, that which they have helped to perpetuate, and in some cases even have helped to create. That is the error or the era of this time you are in now.

Man will choose, whether on astral or physical dimensions, that which he will live with for the next evolutionary cycle of time. That which he has helped to perpetuate and to condone, he will be sentenced with or will be selected to live with for eons of time, as you think of time. Those who have selected the spiritual, the good, the righteous and the light form and have contributed to that will go on in an evolutionary stage of development regarding this planet, the planes surrounding this planet, and the entire solar system. For, as you know, this solar system must evolve in a positive, natural, constructive way for the sons of light to control, to recognize and to come into their rightful heritage as full masters of the cosmic rays and radiations and light force as we have taught and have expressed for millions of years.

So be it in truth. I am Zadkiel of the Sixth Ray, the transmuting and purifying flame of life throughout this solar system and beyond. I work with Uriel, who is of the love, peace, Seventh Ray aspect; interchanging with her, who is of the feminine, this masculine activity of the Sixth Ray when it is feasible, applicable and plausible to do so.

For the Sixth and Seventh Rays are interchangeable during this period of time, depending on what you have earned, depending on how you judge your own thoughts, experiences and evolutionary graces of development for your own specific role and mission in this spiritual time of *now*, the Mark Age period and program for the ongoing of Sananda as the Seventh Ray chohan and the Prince of this planet.

# 4. MANIFESTATION OF LIGHT IN FORM

## REEVOLUTION OF EARTHMAN

Manifestation of light in form is the responsibility of the Fourth Ray function. I, Gabriel, come to herald and to announce this in mankind. All of my endeavors can be traced to the fact that with my appearances and salutations come this phenomenon, to man's way of thinking. But until you are cognizant of, recognize and work with these manipulating energies for the light through third dimensional form, and eventually into the fourth dimensional frequency rate, you will not understand totally what concerns your natural and best interests as sons of the light in this coming era or Aquarian Age.

Yours specifically is to come into higher vibratory familiarities. For you are to express the light in its purest and most magnificent aspects in order to show the evolutionary process of God through matter. You are the sons of God. You are the light, and in the light you are primarily responsible to bring that light out of matter and into its purest, most essential essence, which is Spirit Itself.

Since you are created of spirit and are totally spiritual in nature, but have fallen into matter and have substituted your spiritual natures with other conditions, you now must demonstrate that reevolution process, as we have indicated to you many, many times and have worked with you for eons and ages, beyond your recollection at this time and your appreciation of the processes that are natural to the inheritors of spiritual responsibilities, functions and respects.

We come to you, in this age of marks, as predecessors and protectors. Because we are assigned to this task, many of us in the angelic, celestial realms are fearful to consider the knowledge you may gain and misuse. But we are required to give it, regardless. It subsequently is a matter of conscience on your part and a development or a redevelopment of your reawakening process while you are stimulating the spiritual centers of your own Christ life pat-

41

terns, and required at the same time to eliminate all that you have created out of substance and matter and to recycle it and to put it before you on trial to bring about the true manifestation of your station in life, which is as children of the light and sons of God.

I am ever reminded that this process has been cycled before in other ages and eras and sometimes has failed, as far as the majority of mankind is concerned. But there always have been a few who can comprehend and can accept this tremendous responsibility and this complex knowledge; which is complex only to the mortal, intellectual, reasoning mind and not to the spiritual awareness or Self within. Those minor few have been able to carry the frequency of light into the fourth dimensional consciousness and aspects, creating an etheric realm that is substantiated by the celestial forces and makes ready for the ongoing race as it must evolve from out of the Earth and astral aspects of its evolutionary progress.

## FALL OF MAN

Let us regress here and see what has happened to the race of man since the beginning of time or creation, when he was purely of the light and true essence of God in action. His descent into matter was but an experiment or a period of inquiry. Where he was required to know or to have knowledge, tasting both of the negative and the positive polarities of energy matter, he predominantly became enthralled with that which was of his own creation or ideas, not because he felt that evil or error was better than good or positive action but because he saw that there was an alternate route to all projected positive elements in his creative knowledge of life and life form.

Life form must become a matter of acceptance and control, regardless of the level upon which he works. He must know several areas of expression and be able to express through them in order to gain many multifaceted reasoning and creative principles within himself as a child of the power and the light and the force of good.

But when he expects to control those from the negative elements —in other words, not with the positive control and power projected through him as light and love and life force—he creates within himself and his environment a temporary or substituting series of elements, energies and creative substances. This is the principle of Life Force Itself. And since man is part of Divine Energy and is of a creative principle, he primarily creates as he thinks, as he feels, as he desires, and as he knows the area in which he is experiencing.

42

## ENTRAPMENT ON EARTH

This became the life form on Earth as you now know it, or the third dimensional frequency. In his experiencing and experimentation with this vibratory rate which is known as the planet Earth, he became enmeshed in the series of evolutionary growth patterns or animal-frequency forms and experimented through them for energy, for life, for sensation of the third dimensional frequency, which involves the five senses and the reasoning, intellectual mind.

This power—which is natural unto man, but without the creative spiritual substance of the light and the consciousness of Spirit in him—became more powerful, more attractive in a magnetic sort of way than his own original creation, which was light or form of spiritual substance itself, in its primal energy pattern.

So, the light that is within man, the Christ or cosmic consciousness which is his essence of being, became dimmer and dimmer in the process of becoming more and more enmeshed and concerned with life as it expressed upon the third dimensional plane or planet of Earth as you know it. Environments were created out of this consciousness, which is creative and energizing. Though he would pass from one vehicle into another, he still became entrapped in the sensations and the areas of Earth plane living and evolution.

## TRINITY OF MAN

That is why the astral planes were created. We have astral planes on other planets and spheres in this solar system and elsewhere, also. They are created in the same manner, but not always through negativity or disobedience to the law of life; rather, because they act as subconscious realms or recording contacts for accumulating all the knowledge that is gained on a certain dimension. In those higher areas or more substantially developed areas of life form elsewhere, along with their creative principles of astral realms and energies, the three concepts or trinity aspects are much more controlled from what we call the etheric or spiritual realms of man's expositions.

In other words, he has the ability to control the life force in three levels simultaneously. He can conduct a physical form, as you would call physical; he can tune in or contact a subconscious or astral realm, for picking up or recording all information that has been gained by all of the race in the past during the time of that creative, physical form; and meanwhile, superconsciously or through his I Am Self can conduct these experiments without losing his identity or missing the point of his spiritual origin and being. This is the triune principle in action, outside of this solar system predominantly. In some cases, on the higher planets or planes or spheres of action here, the same does apply.

We are endeavoring to bring this perfection about for the race of man as he now evolves from third dimensional frequency form, or what you call Earth life, into fourth dimensional frequency form, which we term your spiritual or Christ consciousness in action. You will be able to do this before the end of the age called Aquarius by you now, or the next two thousand years; as Sananda, who is and was Jesus the Christ who came to Nazareth through Mary, has been able to return and to come into contact with those children of the light, sons of God, who can adhere to these principles we teach you and prepare you to accept in this present age or the time of *now,* termed by some as the Mark Age period and program.

## SUPERIMPOSITION OF LIGHT BODY

I am heralding this light and this form and this source so you can be prepared properly and can be cognizant of those elements in you which require transmutation and assimilation. In the Fourth Ray function, all must be assimilated, correlated, analyzed and equated with the truth, the light and the frequency for which it is to be balanced and then to be changed.

In the first place, the Fourth Ray represents the true foundation or the foursquare aspects of the four elements that remain on the planet Earth, out of which you have sustained life form for your physical frequency and your life expression in the planetary environment. But as you reach up and out of that foundation and transfer your consciousness into that which is the spiritual energy, light and form, you must be able to stand on that knowledge and control in order to lift yourself beyond that stage or level of evolvement.

Since you descended into matter in a very gradual and scientific manner, you must do the same when leaving that matter or form. You will not create a new body out of the physical body, but you will superimpose the light body over the physical body and will absorb it or will dissolve it, in time incorporating it with the light frequency which is all in all.

In other words, the light frequency or light body, which we term the resurrected form of life substance, is all energy, is all form, is all matter that exists in and through this solar system. So, it is quite capable, as Spirit in action or spiritual form in action, to absorb or to dissolve the lower energies or frequencies which exist and are represented by the four lower elements of your physical body and consciousness, represented by the rational mind and by the conscious and subconscious selves.

You are not two or three self-consciousnesses. You are one consciousness, which is your light body, your Christ understanding and your spiritual identity as an I-Am-that-I-Am concept. Out of this I Am or Jehovah consciousness, as you might call it, is the contact or connection with cosmic Self or spiritual energy and primeval force.

## MANIPULATION OF ENERGY

Life, energy and matter are one, and are in One Which is God or Spirit. That must become your total experience and knowledge at this time. For without it you will not be able to create and to control all of these elements and purposes of which we now are speaking and to which I herald your attention and bring about a new dispensation and life adventure.

When you come through this consciousness and realize that you are to begin to manipulate this energy from its primeval force and source, you then will know the power and the love that are combined in the First and the Seventh Rays as they express through you in your own evolving grace and growth.

But until that time comes you must take our instructions and adhere to our principles and give yourselves the opportunities to consider all of these many messages and conceptional relationships and formulas we must give you in order to awaken your consciousness, spiritually speaking, on the Earth plane and planet at this time. It is not necessary for you to take down these formulas and procedures in a mathematical way, because your conscious mind and rationalizing intellect cannot comprehend all that is inherent in these teachings and in these exercises.

## AWAKENING OF EARTHMAN

But what it does do is open the spiritual consciousness to go to work within you and to record and to remind you of all those things which are inherent in your knowledge and are part of your spiritual heritage. This ever has been the purpose of higher plane activity and the teachings of the etheric masters and the celestial forces who come to man at this time to restimulate that which is as a seed dormant within his conscious and subconscious mind aspects. He is awake, it is true. He is responding, it is true. But he cannot control these things from the mortal or the subconscious, which is the astral or the soul level of his functioning and familiarities.

When I speak to you of these matters I reawaken certain intricate mathematical recollections that are inbuilt in the spiritual consciousness or the I Am Self, who knows and who works with and who reorganizes all of the life force in you, regardless of whether it expresses on the physical as a material matter and form or body or whether it is in the subconscious, soul aspect; which in itself also has a form or body of expression, a vehicle, so to speak. That vehicle operates between lives or incarnations. Sometimes, as you know, in the evolutionary process you as a soul will return unto a physical form or a dimension in order to incorporate and to pick up further material or knowledge.

In other instances you may be released from your soul recordings and go back into the etheric realms and relive and restimulate those etheric or spiritual contacts and expressions for a short period of time before returning unto your spiritual mission, which may express outwardly on a third dimensional plane or an astral plane or outside of your contact with the solar system in which you are presently involved.

These experiences all are recorded in the subconscious or astral mind, which we call the soul aspect of man and which is the most important aspect of your awakening process in the present era or time of *now;* because without its cooperation you may not progress and may not make the total union with the higher Self or Christ within for the demonstration that is required in order to dissolve the physical, or to rebuild the physical according to spiritual principles upon which it should have been built and have been maintained in the first place.

## ORIGIN OF MAN ON EARTH

Let me give you an example of how this may operate. This also is an example of what did take place in the beginning or genesis of your time on Earth, since you have it recorded in many scriptural references, regardless of race or religion you may be inclined to follow at this time.

Man in his true spiritual evolution, when recording a finding of life sequences, was attracted unto the planet as you now know it, a third dimensional, physical, elementary origin of life substances and concepts. It was meant to be a house unto which certain animal and vegetable kingdoms were to develop and to experience higher life form. But because mankind—as you know, a son of God

46

or the Light—came into responsible governing sharings, he substituted the plan and the principle by incorporating his own energy frequency in those animal forms.

He first introduced himself to those beasts of the field in which you now have mammoth constructions and structures. But this was so unsuitable to any manipulation of the area in which he was confined that he soon dissolved any interest in those beasts of the field. As many of the legends and prerecorded memory patterns remain and since are left upon the planet in legendary form, you could recall these and resort to them for reference, if need be.

But when he began to desire a control over all these lower beasts and to use the energy sources on the planet for his own manipulations and clarifications, he took an animal form that was more conducive to expansion and experimentation and rested his spiritual light force within it; which is a possibility and a prerogative of the higher energy forces, such as the light body or the spiritual, resurrected form of which we are speaking.

By introducing himself into those animal forms, not one or two at a time but whole groups of them, he became involved in the evolutionary pattern of those forms and he sustained life for more than the period of time recommended for such. These contacts remained longer and longer and these controls became more involved in the ensuing periods when Earth was very primitive and very convulsed in its own equilibrium and contracting expansions.

As we became more concerned with this aspect or level of man's involvement and interest in the three-dimensional form as it was contracting, we became less and less able to extract and to control and to convince man in the ethereal form about the magnetic attraction of his concentration upon these four lower elements: earth, air, water and light.

The light within or the spiritual consciousness, derived from his own primal source or God sense, became less involved or concerned with his experience than with the lower elements relating to the planet and its problems and complexities. In other words, the body which man took on related more closely, in his interests, to that which he was experiencing at that time than to the spiritual consciousness with which he totally should have been concerned, involved in and in control of.

But because the communication of his spiritual or light-body Self was less and less with that of the celestial planes which control the lower elements and work with them, he and the celestial forces or angelic realms became less and less in contact or rapport.

Man is involved in the form and the mathematical formula of that form only to the extent that he can keep control of his spiritual consciousness during the time it is evolving and is contracting itself to or adhering to the other elements and the other forms with the area or the sequence of events which are unfolding; because in evolution and in experiment of energy with all the elements that are involved in that energy, he has a certain relationship and a certain responsibility, but may not supersede his responsibility over the general cosmic plan, program and procedure of that time, that place and that part of the evolutionary graduations.

Man comes in contact with the elements of the environment in which he is involved or is supposed to have some control and some supervision. For man is a governor of life energy force and a controller or co-creator with light substance. Therefore, he enters into form because he is supposed to manipulate, to know and to create a series of evolutionary steps that can bring that form into a higher refinement and transmute it into spiritual essence, making it subject to his will and knowledge, provided it is for the higher good of that form and that area.

All of these things are true and good throughout time. There are many areas which man will discover and will know about from his own past evolutionary processes and because he will go into them in future times as he gains this knowledge and recaptures his spiritual purpose as it was from the beginning.

But for now we look upon this in a negative and positive polarity aspect. The positive polarity of Creative Energy is the idea. The negative polarity of Spirit or Energy is the acting-out upon that Energy Force or within that Energy Force so that it creates a third or material substance, a realization of the positive and negative polarities in action together, simultaneously and equally balanced.

Therefore, when man as a son of God enters into matter or form, he is to act upon it and through it as a spiritual being. In so doing he is to reconstitute its elements into that which is for his higher understanding and fulfillment. But until he can create a spiritual awareness within that form, he is merely mismanaging and destroying the spiritual or initial intention of his creative principles which are to keep balanced with the two sources or forces within himself: positive and negative polarities of the God Force or spiritual Sonship.

Man has been experimenting in this manner for ages upon the Earth. Now must come the remembrance of that procedure in himself so he can control that force and keep it in a perfect balance and reconstitute those energies as they originally were intended. This is the process he is going through at the present time.

## RENEWAL OF EARTH LIFE

Whether or not all are going to be able to come into this awareness at one time is not essentially the point or the whole matter. The important thing is that a sufficient number, who are required to do this, become light, love and life force, reconstituted, rebalanced and reformulated according to the basic principle of their spiritual intention and life-energy responsibilities.

In this process those who are so elected, because they select themselves, to do this will teach, will bring about a new form in the Earth and through their fellowmen who are so entrapped in this lesser consciousness and lower form and are hypnotized by the magnetic energy they themselves have created of what you call third dimensional form, and will not remain there when this is properly executed.

We in angelic realms, particularly those under the Fourth Ray aspect I speak of, can do this because we have helped to formulate or to crystallize these energy patterns in man when he became so enmeshed and promiscuous in his manipulation of the four lower elements, becoming thus a human form or an animal form with a spiritual consciousness within.

The light form, or the spiritual consciousness of that light form, can renew and reestablish what has been. For it is in the record, the subconscious or soul-memory pattern, how to do this. We bring this about through our various elements of the Fourth Ray concepts by reminding you of the process through which you came into material matter form via your own spiritual will and concepts, to begin with. For you create at all times. You created this form. You created this life pattern. You created the life history of this planet as it is unfolding now. And you can re-create it, reenergize it, reformulate it, and rejuvenate yourselves in the process.

## REJUVENATION OF EARTHMAN

The rejuvenation of which we speak, of course, is the rejuvenation of your higher Self or your spiritual intention as it was supposed to magnify itself in time through this planetary sphere and over all the elements of this planetary sphere at the origin of its time and place in the conceptional period when the Earth planet

49

was formed and all elements and life form were introduced to it. But you did not choose to do this. Now you must choose to do this, by the recollection, the restitution and the re-forming of that which was to be, and is to be, rebalanced.

You see, you cannot circumvent ever divine law, divine decree and the divine evolutionary pattern as it is set forth from the Godhead or Energy Source Itself. You must go on. You must remember that regardless of how long you take, regardless of what mistrials and what misfortunes and what misadventures and paths you have taken and thus have averted the divine will, the divine decree, the divine plan, you eventually must come full face to confront this, to work with it and to come about the business of doing our Father's will. You are now at that stage of evolution.

You may not understand how, in two hundred and six million years of creative energy force and evolvement of a planet such as Earth, you can make up for or rebalance, re-form, everything that has taken place in that period of time. But you will come to know, to understand and to recognize that God's will be done, no matter how long it takes or how many energies, forces and creations of God are called into play in order to complete that plan, design and scheme of Divine Energy and the mind of God as It creates Its own purposes and developments. For eras and ages are as nothing unto this cosmic scheme and planetary expression.


## OTHER FORMS

Yours is but a happening in a tremendous, dramatic episode of total and eternal ongoing. Rest assured that there are many plans and schemes by which this may work itself out in the process of evolution. But because you are familiar with one form or another is no reason to think it is the only form through which you have passed as sons of God. You see, there also are other forms which you know not of and recognize not and will experience, and have experienced in the past.

Just as we have prepared you to know and to accept the fact that you may be in contact mentally and spiritually with a form called creative energy as expresses through the angelic kingdoms, but see them not, they exist nevertheless and are in good standing with you, respecting your free will and your desire to experiment and to experience life form and source as you will it.

But that is not my choice. It is yours to make, singularly and alone; while ours is to conduct a racial concept and a total pattern of an entire segment of God's creation which is mankind or the

50

Son of the Light, co-creators with our God pattern and God intention. You may not know how this interrelationship works at this particular time. But again, that is of no consequence to us, or even to yourselves at this point in your evolution and in the unfolding of the pattern which you now are expressing as sons of God.

## RETURN TO SONSHIP

You must come to know and come to accept the fact that you have many evolutionary steps to relive, to re-form and to recall as you go on from mortal existence and come back into the true spiritual consciousness from which you originally were conceived and from which you fell into this matter or mortal being.

As reiterated many times in the past, it is not the other way around. You are not mortal; or not created out of the substances and the elements of a planetary accident, then developing a consciousness that can evolve itself into something that is spiritualized. A whole new concept must be given to man, one which he knows well from within himself because he suspects it and because it happens to be the truth. But until enough men on the Earth can sufficiently sustain this knowledge and accept this principle and work with it in a correlating, cooperative, coordinated manner, you will have absolutely no success whatsoever.

It is not a cohesive principle which you as an individual can control or can work with from the Godhead. For the Godhead or the Divine Principle Which created the race intact as an entire concept or idea out of Itself, totally balanced negative and positive polarities of spiritual energy in form, is substantially and primarily concerned with the fact that that form or idea which we call mankind or Son of the Light must work as a cohesive whole and not as individual parts of that whole, for the good of the whole or for the good of any individual.

Although many individuals of that whole have conceived of the total project and prospect of restating and reinstating the Sonship principle of mankind in the third dimensional frequency form of material matter, they have not been able to sustain substantially that concept and that principle with any lasting effect for any good or appreciable period of time.

Yes indeed, there have been great and magnificent moments in the history of mankind since he fell into matter. Great souls have come upon the Earth and have promoted these principles and have brought forth these ideals and have reminded mankind, in his own soul evolutionary process, of his original purpose and concept.

But because so much evil and error concept have grown out of his error ways and negative principles of manipulating matter and energy, thus creating a mortal being, a mortal body and a mortal concept of life energy force, he has not been able to step out of that mortal concept and creation of his own making and to come back into his spiritual origin, powers, talents and faculties, as he must do in the Aquarian Age ahead.

## THE 144,000

Therefore, in order to insure this problem and process we reorganize the entire situation, to infuse the light, the truth and the matter of spiritual form in matter through a hundred and forty-four thousand light workers demonstrating and manipulating this energy matter or light bodies simultaneously upon the Earth in order to create a strong enough force field by which all matter upon the Earth frequency can come into its true spiritual balance and control during these latter days, and then into the next two thousand years of time, as you record it, approximately.

Now we seek those who will adhere to this principle and can reconstitute the light matter or the light-frequency force of the spiritualized thinking, memories and reasoning powers of the mind matter and make a new man out of that which originally was.

Spirit is in action in each one. Spirit in you can adhere to the Spirit in all. Therefore, in this unity of spiritual action, spiritual dedication and spiritual thoughtfulness, powers and concepts we make a new planet, a new life form for all the species involved on that planet, as well as bring every single God's son into his true heritage and role upon the Earth planet in these latter days.

That must be the entire purpose and program toward which you are dedicated. For without that single-minded dedication of all one hundred and forty-four thousand light workers working together, we cannot hope for the success that must come about in the next period of time we call the Mark Age program. Amen. So be it in truth. This is Gabriel of the Fourth Ray aspect bringing about a new basis and foundation and heralding the light as it must express outwardly in the fourth phase of the rending of the seventh veil. So be it. Om.

# 5. CREATION OF FORM

## LAWS OF PRECIPITATION

We will teach you about the creation of form out of matter. This is Jophiel of the Second Ray, under the Elohim of thought and intelligence, mind, which creates matter from the energy principle which is the source of all things. God is all that is, and in Him or It, Which is Creative Substance, come all the aspects, the elements and the activities which are divine, unchangeable and spiritual law.

It is based on mathematical precision, as you would think in terms of scientific exactness. Yet, as it works upon this science and is unchangeable by this law of scientific expression, using your terminologies again, we know and project that you yourselves, mankind on Earth, will become more convinced and able to create the forms which you desire in your own lives.

As we speak we precipitate these laws into action; and hope and trust, and protect you, that you will use this spiritual, scientific formula to bring about that desired result in your own lives for the good of all that comes under your influence, just as it is the purpose of Divine Mind through Creative Energy to bring about that justice and truth and spiritual equality for all things which come under Its dominion and are part of It and inseparable from It.

## SEVEN RAYS OF LIFE

The first law or light of God is energy. This is represented by the masculine aspect. It is the idea to create, to be. Under the Elohim or the aspect of God which is this first law and light, I recommend the Archangel Michael.

From the second aspect comes Jophiel, the archangel of thought or mind in motion, creating and bringing forth the third, which is love, the love of God which descended through the self projection, Midas-Lucifer, the light who was replaced by the Archangel Chamuel.

This triune action had manifested, had crystallized and had equaled the fourth. For the two primary aspects, which are Father-Mother God, masculine-feminine polarities, creating love, developed a fourth true and sound form in matter. My colleague here is Gabriel, the archangel of the Fourth Ray or aspect.

This foundation or these four corners create or sustain all life form throughout all universes. But standing upon this foursquare, we put the unity of purpose and the integrating of all these principles under the Fifth Ray or aspect. Raphael is the archangel under the Elohim of integrating substance and thought, activity and love. Building upon this, we then transmute, refine and purify all that has been gained and has been gathered by this activity, this thought.

The sixth aspect of God in action is the transmuting flame. By Zadkiel's sovereignty we come to the seventh, and here is Uriel, which completes all that has gone before it. Upon this triune principle or pyramid we stand foursquare and a triune: light, law, love. Nothing else is needed.

If you can understand all of these principles involved, the aspects of God in and through all creation—divine law, and love and light combined upon a solid foundation of the first four activities—you yourselves can create any idea, any principle, any love and bring it into full manifestation and spiritualized creativity. Let this ever be your law in practice. Let this ever be your procedure.


## LEARNING TO CREATE FORM

In past discourses we have brought to your attention the essential fact that the archangels are only in charge of the thought, the forms which you create and are created for us to hold intact. Until you are capable of doing this and holding forth this solid object in the procedure which I have outlined for you, I cannot guarantee that anywhere or any time you will be able to be without this protective hierarchal plan, of others substituting for you and governing over your development.

But this is not as it was originally created or seen. As you will learn in time, you have been created with the substance and the consciousness. In-built within your creative principle of Sonship is this right and heritage, lost in past eras and times, but to be regained when you have learned the sum and the substance of divine laws and the ability to precipitate them and to create from them the matter and the form that are suitable and equitable to all living things, governed with justice and mercy but above all with the love of God predominant.

Since the love of God was turned against or away from God towards self, which was the individualization of a part of God, the Sonship, then we have this responsibility, in the aspects of our being true to the divine principles and the spiritual laws, to act for and in place of that which temporarily has been lost or has been deceived.

In man's evolution he comes to recognize the principles of spiritual law as it affects his material life and his own creative energies from within. If only he will apply these in every instance to his own fulfillments and his own understandings of himself, we shall gain the purpose for which we all are concentrating in these end times of Earth planetary structure.

## MANIFESTING DIVINE IDEAS

We have said we would teach you how to create form. You already have the mathematical precision presented here. But, as I have indicated, it is through the Second Ray of Intelligence and Wisdom—which is the feminine aspect or the Mother aspect of the duality of God; starting with the first principle, which is light—that we understand now the Second Ray involvement and creative discipline.

Thought and ideas of good are ever inward and exciting to all parts of the tributaries of God light and truth, which is the first principle. So, as these ideas are emanating out of the Godhead—the principles of justice and beauty, equality, helpfulness and compassion, duty and the practice of discipline—we see them then picked up by every aspect of creation, particularly those who are the sons of the Light and the ideas or the Mind Which creates them. While these emanating ideas reach the consciousness individually of those individualizations or sons of God who are the sons of Light Itself, we see them grow and expand in a desire to bring about form and expression.

This then, you see, is how the first four aspects work together. First there are light and truth and law. Second is the idea emanating out from the mind of God as thoughts and principles; which are picked up by the third aspect, this great love or Son, which already is in Self-form or Self-realization identity under the Third Ray aspect. These three acting together, fusing together, melding and working together, create the fourth: desire for manifestation.

55

The desire and the feeling that come from mind, thought, law, light bring about the fourth aspect of manifestation or form. Each one of the archangels perpetrates, protects and circulates part of this energy which we call the light body or the light form, clothing it and bringing it into a reality to be utilized and functioning. For the individualizations are those of the Fourth Ray, which often is called the crystallization or manifestation aspect.

This, as said before, is not only the principle by which you personally work in bringing forth your own ideas in material form, but is actually how it works throughout the eons of time in invisible energy perpetuation until there is a form that can be utilized by the various individuals or individual creations of the Godhead.

## IDEALS ARE NOT PERSONALITIES

Let us look at the principle of beauty and see that this then can become various forms of art, architecture, and the enhancement of one's own physical form or manifested body wherever it might be expressing. This, though, is an idea, a principle, and not an individualization. Because these ideals have worked through all of the divine principles involved and are expressed out by all of the angelic realm, many erroneously have put identities or personalities around them; seeking, saying, and falsely identifying them, as creations with aspects and destinies of their own; able to express, let us say, through a personality expression.

So, you have some who claim that freedom speaks or is or works as an identity or a personality; purity speaks and works and has an identity; love speaks, has thoughts and has an identity. Surely this is not so, from the aspect of man taking upon himself a form and a personality, or an individualized creation such as we; who, though we do not work in the personality aspect that man does, have identities and work in group form in realms that are beyond your particular comprehension at this time, having activities that are unrelated to those activities with which you are familiar in the societies and the congregations or the groups with which you are involved.

But these generalized aspects or ideals cannot have personalities or identities of their own, though the ideals themselves are real enough because they come from the Second Ray realm of ideas in Divine Mind, or the Mother aspect of the dual polarity of the Godhead, the negative principle from the positive energy, light and law.

56

# DUAL ASPECT OF MAN

My purpose in bringing this to your attention is so that you may clothe your ideas and ideals with as much substance as some erroneously have clothed their own higher aspirations and goals, too. But before you do this you must clarify within yourself the function of the Godhead, yourselves as the Son or the creation of that Godhead, and the lower principles by which you perform your functions and must bring into solidified effect a manifested product based on a spiritualized idea.

For this is the dual aspect of the sons of God in physical form. They must bring about the manifested foursquare principle upon which to rest the trinity aspect or pyramid. The pyramid of the triune Self rests squarely on the four aspects of the lower form, and only by raising it up and having a triune spiritualized Self-structure can man hope to complete his mission in the third dimensional world or physical life on Earth and be expressing in his fourth dimensional body or resurrected light form, which is the Christ aspect or the eternal Self.

The mortal self, which rests on material matter, is raised only by erecting the triune structure of the immortal Self, the personality and the identity of his original creation from the Godhead. Thus the complexity of the mathematical formula which I have given; because it is from the wisdom aspect, the intellect which you have had created for you in order to work out these things and to sustain you through these difficult periods; but on the other hand acts as a very subtle and cunning trap to keep you from spiritualizing those very ideas through that very mind or intellect, the reasoning powers that were given to you for you to work this through.

In other words, it is that you must work out these divine principles through that aspect of yourself which is related to Divine Mind. From Divine Mind you have had created an intellectual and reasoning mind which, turned around and turned in upon your self-interests, self-glory, self-satisfactions, have kept you trapped and enmeshed in material matter, out of which you now must climb via the same mind and the same reasoning and the same thought patterns.

It is true that love is the key. But you are love, you are that aspect of Divine Mind and divine law which is love. And love is the Son of God, the feeling nature of this dual principle of negative and positive polarity. The Divine Mind is negative polarity, the law of God and the truth of light are the positive polarity, creating this third aspect which is the Sonship or creative principle. That is what we call the Third Ray aspect. Again, as I have said, you will be given this information through Chamuel.

## BUILD NEW FOUNDATION

When you are through searching, analyzing, seeking and pulling apart all of these analytical concepts, twisting and turning them in your thought patterns, you still will come up with the same mathematical formulas which have been given here simply and directly, and eternally from the beginning of time.

You are not to be blamed entirely for this search, for you were created with this searching mind and with these intellectual, analytical capabilities. But because of them you have hindered your own growth simply because you did not use the principles involved that were there for you to use since the beginning of time, and for all time, in order to build a more substantial and more worthy cause than you have built in the mortal world as you now know it and as you have created it of yourself.

You have been told time and time again through your spiritual teachers and instructors that what you have created you must face and work with and suffer through. This is so true, and this is the problem of man in these coming days ahead. That which you as a race have created upon this plane and planet you now must deal with and dissolve, re-create from that same energy—transmute it, so to speak—in these latter days or transmuting ray aspects and bring about a new foundation upon which to build, which must be the spiritual light-form or body.

Since you have been given these principles now, and the creative aspects upon which to build these principles, and since you now have been brought to a peak in your own spiritual understanding through trial and error, you now can build foursquarely that which is everlastingly true and right and just, that which is the spiritual body, on a solid foundation, regarding the physical plane and planet known as Earth.

Jesus the Christ, of course, has demonstrated this already for you by building in your midst, and out of the substances which you have within your orbit consciousness and out of the elements with which you are concerned and working, a spiritual body that was created and sustained, transmuted and ascended, out of this plane.

58

When he reintroduces that same superstructure or spiritual body onto the same plane—because you will have created a force field strong enough for him to reintroduce it, and those who have created that force field for him to reintroduce it have sustained their own light body on that physical structure or plane known as Earth—you then will be able to transmute the entire planet, all life upon the planet, and to rebuild that which originally was intended for you to keep, to sustain and to work with on this planetary structure known as Earth, or third dimensional frequency matter.

## CO-CREATORS WITH GOD

Now that you know this is part of your purpose and you have been instructed as how to work with it, you are required, naturally, and are held in the strictest responsibility, to bring it about. This is where the mind energy, the thoughts, the ideals and the goals of the Second Ray will sustain you. This is where I as Jophiel will continue to aid you.

Let me give you this as an example. Although all ideas and great ideals come from Divine Mind Itself—since all that is good comes from God and is God, was created by God—and you who are part of God therefore are picking up these thoughts, these energies, these ideals, these purposes, we still see them as interacting, and hold you responsible for co-creating with God a solid foundation in which they can come into substantial matter. That is your responsibility as a co-creator with God. That which God sends out or idea sends out to you, and you pick up and work with, you then must demonstrate as a co-creator and bring into its full fruition, for that is your function.

The Second Ray aspect, or the angels upon this aspect of the Second Ray under myself, work with this energy, hold this energy intact. For, as we said before, the purpose of the angelic kingdom is to keep the radiating principles of light and life in the proper perspective and balance with a light form; or, if you want to use the term, spiritual form.

This spiritual form is beyond what you consider form, for it does not take on substance until you give it the further energy out of the love aspect and the crystallization or the Fourth Ray aspect that you put into it. But it must pass through your feeling and desire and love for creation, and as a co-creator, to bring it into manifested principle or growth.

59

## FORMULATION AND SPIRITUALIZATION

The archangel of the Second Ray is responsible for holding this ideal in perspective so that you as sons of God pick it up, work with it and make a creative principle out of it; taking all the three preceding steps, adding the fourth step, and then making it into some substantial activity. This requires the Archangels Michael, Jophiel, Chamuel, who replaced Lucifer, and Gabriel. When this becomes real, in the sense of an active force in your collective lives as a race wherever you might be incarnating or congregating, then we have completed that particular truth.

It may be on an etheric realm, it may be on another planet other than what you now know, it may be through space and time, before it can be idealized, formulated. When it is formulated it must be spiritualized sufficiently that it returns unto the Godhead from Which it was originally inspired. So, again you have the foursquare principle or crystallization completion with the integrating principles of everything you have been involved in and have been working with, wherever this may be.

You purify or refine, burning off any extraneous dross or complicated, unwanted energy, thought, activity that was involved, until this has become its most pure state again. Then you rest upon that, with its spiritual fullness completed; the seven steps of precipitating an original idea or energy coming from God, working down through whatever matter and form you are permitted to use, and supplying the love of your own creative rights as parts of God, His co-creators in eternity. For this privilege, for this learning, for this experiencing God Self within you, you are rewarded, though it take a good part of your eternal existence.

## DIVINE IDEALS AND GOALS

Until you learn to do this perfectly and properly, you will be searching, growing, yearning and discontented. It is this divine discontent within you which you find so stimulating and which urges you to move forward and to change that which is in your life pattern and in your experience wherever you are, throughout time and space.

It is, let us say, endless. For the ideals that come from the Godhead are far beyond anything you have comprehended or have picked up so far in your Earth plane existence. Indeed yes, you have come up with some really exceptional goals and missions. To name just a few, as we already have: beauty, equality, freedom, mercy, compassion; gifts all of God. But these are only a few of the first golden gems which are in your eternal existence and realization as spiritual beings.

You have thought, for ages and ages upon the Earth plane itself and through the magnificence of philosophical and spiritualized thinking of your religious leaders and spiritual thinkers and philosophers, that these golden gems of ideas are the highest goals man could yearn for and achieve. In fact, some of you say it is so utopian that they cannot even be realized or completed on this plane and planet, for man will not permit it, he is so filled with other ideas and negations of these principles and ideals.

But you know not of the greater and the grander ideals and purposes and goals which lie ahead. These are but the childish toys of an awakening man; of man, a race of giants, that can conceive only of the first perfections of a spiritualized life. They are but the scratchings of the surface of your higher goals, ambitions and life substance.

But because they are important and because they are the beginning and because they are so essential and important to the foundation of your spiritualized being, we say to you: they must be fulfilled, they must be worked out upon this plane and planet where you have picked up these ideals and have brought them through from the Originator of them, Which is God; idea, mind and energy of good for all equally.

So, we begin, of course, where we are. We begin at the beginning. These ideals which are coming to you from the Godhead, sustained and held in form for you by the ray of the second aspect of God—or the Elohim of thought, intelligence and mind matter— we see that you in your own aspects of idealized thinking can complete them and bring them forth for yourselves as a race, for all life upon the planet, to bring the planet into its final fruition as a spiritualized aspect and creation. So, with this goal in mind and with this aspect so clearly defined for you, we now close and complete this transmission. Jophiel.

# 6. CREATION BY THOUGHT

## SEVEN LAYERS OF SEVEN ASPECTS

Let us continue to examine the creation of form out of the substance and energy which are thought. I am Jophiel, working in and through Nada, the supreme consciousness of the channel here known as Yolanda of the Sun. It is important that we understand these various levels and conscious applications of the spiritual, divine, creative substance of light, life, form, because if we do not understand this we cannot understand the manipulation of this energy and we will not be able to advance in our specific practices, which are: to eliminate the error consciousness and the error thought forms which have taken on substantial life form and energy, and to create the higher aspects of our specific roles and missions in eternal existence.

Your predominant possibilities for the incoming New Age of Aquarius are performing these things with conscious spiritual, scientific or mathematical precision designed for you, prepared by you and executed within your dominion of light, life, love form in the fourth dimensional frequency body known as the light or resurrected spiritual development. I am come to enhance these things through your own intellectual will or knowledge.

There are seven aspects to man. There are seven aspects to Creative Energy as expressing through man. There are seven layers of each one of those aspects you have been given and have been asked to conquer, to work with and to express through. These are so multifaceted, the multiplicity of them is so complex, the rewards are so satisfying that we can only begin to shed light and knowledge on some, but not all.

For in doing it for one aspect, which we shall do here, in essence we shall do it for all the other aspects, because you yourselves will be able to apply divine rule and logic that are meant here for yourselves as you go on and need to apply them and to work them out specifically in your own roles and missions, aspects and developments.

Since I am the archangel of the Second Ray, and this is the aspect and condition of mind in matter through form, we examine minutely and carefully what is implied here by the seven layers of multiplicities. In the raw, essential, primal energy force of God as expressed through the Elohim of the second aspect and the second step of consciousness, mind is light. It is the unfolding, the working, the understanding of energy or life force which needs to be expressed or in motion. This is the thought realm. In creating those thoughts we have wisdom or understanding. This is the superconscious or etheric realm of man, the second layer of primal source.

Intelligence is that which is working in the unfolding of wisdom, or the third aspect or layer of Divine Mind in action. Understanding is the fourth, that which expresses in the mortal realm or the physical development of mankind. The fifth, intellectual or reasoning powers, relates to the conscious and to the brain as it has evolved from this planetary sphere.

The sixth is logic or factual reasoning, but not the working out of new ideas; the responding only to that which is given to it by others. The seventh, the subconscious storehouse, is merely the memory of mental activity as it may have been given to you personally or to any other of the race during its inhabitation of the area where mankind may reside.

These seven levels within the one aspect give you a comprehensive but not complete understanding of the grades and the relationships you have to work through mind manipulation, mind power and spiritual law attached to that aspect. If you cannot apply any one of these areas, or many of these areas, to what we will bring to your attention at this time, you cannot understand all the many other aspects and functions you are required to bring to pass while we unfold these powers and bring you into contact with the light function of Divine Mind Itself.

But before we begin, let us understand and accept the fact that all this is in-built in your consciousness area by area slowly so you can call upon the reservoir of knowledge that is there. Again, this applies to the Second Ray aspect of knowledge, understanding, wisdom and thought power.

## FROM THOUGHT TO FORM

Man is a son of God, a creation in himself, divinely projected from the source of life, which is the law of God, the word and the idea, then put into motion and then manifested out through the love of this dual but single force. Man then has the capability of thinking within that Divine Mind or Energy. He sees, senses, knows what is in divine property itself. Therefore, he selects a single aspect of that, a thought, and contemplates it. Again, this refers to the mental activity. Nothing has been formed as yet.

While this thought process is expanding and growing, other properties, aspects and conditions of his divine nature are correlating to it and conceiving within it an area of expression, an area of exploration, a response to it. According to how purely and dramatically this activity resolves itself within the mind of the race of man, or a majority of the race of man, wherever it may be contemplating this thought, a form takes place.

We of the angelic kingdoms, the celestial realm, responding to this activity are concerned with the elements that record what has been contemplated. A substance is created from this activity of thought and contemplation, and molecules of energy patterns, which we call elements, become attracted to one another and adhere to one another in varying degrees, complexities and formulas. No two are alike. For no two thoughts are ever the same, regardless of how often they are dwelt upon or determined by the individuals who bring them to pass or who decide upon that single effort.

You must understand this takes eons and ages of time to develop, and much in the way of trial and error is conducted. Many things are thought and contemplated and worked upon which never do take on substance and form or have any creation of themselves as individuals or identities.

### COMPREHENSION OF SONSHIP

It is this process which is the natural and inherent privilege of man as a co-creator, as a son of God. What does it mean to be a son of God or a child of this perfection which is all that there is, all that ever has been and all that ever shall be? It means to be the sum and the substance of all that is, all that ever has been and all that ever can be. It means to have within it all the properties, the consciousnesses and the responsibilities.

But being the son, one can never be the Father and the Mother. One is always the product of the activities, the consciousness and the primary source of that Originator. It means that you never can be the originator of energy or the source of life, light and love, for you are the product of this triune essence.

Yet, within that triune essence you have all that is, all that ever was and all that ever can be. Learning how to use it, learning how to apply it and learning to become it in its fullest extent and in its

64

varied multiplicities is more than you have learned to cope with, even unto this age and time and place and scheme of things.

For we are created of the Source and are never the Source Itself. This *we* applies to your realms and creation as a son as well as to ours, which include the angelic, the devic and the elemental forces, regarding all life planes, existences, forms everywhere and throughout all eternity.

Being the son and having this power of thought, co-creating in Divine Mind what has been thought and is being thought, combining these elements, crystallizing them, decrystallizing them, manifesting them, demanifesting them will take eternity in order to explore every mathematical equation and potential, will it not?

Should it not be the total concern of mankind as he evolves from grace to grace and talent to talent and comprehension to higher comprehension? Comprehending the power of his own being is the purpose of mankind. And so he goes from area to area, evolutionary process or form to the next step, in this ongoing privilege.

## THOUGHT FORMS

The thought form we have mentioned, over which all angelic beings are in charge, concerns the relationship of man with the other elements or the other forces in the creative principalities of the Godhead so that he, mankind, can understand and can work with all of these interrelating substances and consciousnesses who have come to aid, to work with and to complement his force, his purpose and his destiny as a son of the Light and a child of God Force.

That we are not the creators of these thought forms but the aspect which keeps them in their rightful balance, design and position is all we can contribute to the creative principles and the spiritual laws in action as they occur, develop, and dematerialize in the wake of new forms or materializations to come.

When a series of thoughts is strong enough and powerful enough to make a certain specific legion of themselves—which you might call a species or a concept, depending on the level of the thought projection—our efforts are to keep it intact as long as it is recorded by the minds of men and developed by the thoughts and the feelings they put into that thought form.

## CONCEPTS ARE NOT FORMS

We have drawn your attention to the fact that there are concepts as well as actual specific forms; or species, as we have called them.

65

Because these concepts are part of your evolvement and development as sons of God, we must bring to your attention that a concept is not a thing in the same respect that a form of life or material-object species is.

Let us look at the difference between the concept of love and compassion for one's fellowmen as opposed or in relationship to an animal form that is for the comfort, the protection and the expression of love by a physical aspect of mankind upon a particular plane or planet. Yes indeed, you have animal forms you even have not dreamt of or have not seen consciously with your personality incarnated mind on Earth, but have experienced on other planes and planets. Some of these animal forms or purposes are picked up by you in dream, vision and imagination through the conscious personality aspects of Earth plane consciousness. Some of them exist in fairy tales, myths and legends.

But a concept of love and compassion for one's fellow being is not a form which has a life pattern existing independently from man's thinking process, mental activities and understandings on the seven multiple ways of approaching divine thought, energy and pattern as here outlined in the beginning of this chapter.

You must come to comprehend, to separate, to conceive of these varying thought patterns. Is one a species unlike any other, that, once projected out from your creative thought pattern, has an existence and a life form unattached to you independently? Does the concept of love and compassion for one's fellow beings exist only when you think about and act upon it; or does it have an existence outside, separate and independent from, your thinking patterns and intellectual scope of workings? This you must come to understand.

But the fact remains that man has created both at one time or another in his divine existence and purposes. In the beginning and in the pure state of evaluating these things man has helped to create both the concept and the life energy form of various species with which he has relationship in one area or another of his multiplicities of expression.

## MULTIPLICITIES OF MAN'S EXPRESSION

Let us review the multiplicities of expression man has before him and the opportunities he has in which to express these multiplicities of expression. He exists as an idea in the Divine Mind of the dual Force: positive and negative mind, life, energy. This is before his individualizations and personalities take form. He exists in the

66

Sonship concept of Divine Mind as a creation, a total being in which he is part of the trinity of God's activity and force and purpose.

He exists in his individualization within that Sonship, which is his Christ Self. Out of that Christ Self he has what we call the light body or the resurrected form. For the light body is resurrected out of the material form man has created from this power, energy, understanding and love he has for his triune purpose in the God-head.

He has the ability to create a form out of this divine conscious-ness or Sonship, the Christ Self; and has done so in many places, times and eras. But as far as the Earth planet is concerned, let us realize he has developed a soul counterpart to this Sonship or Christ Self which records every experience and adventure in which he has participated. Out of this soul form he then has material form and matter on the Earth plane. For he has thought and has created this by descending into the elements to which he has been attracted in eons past.

From this we have the subconscious memory patterns in the brain that evolved and developed in order to house all these experi-ences and to give an opportunity for the form to express intelli-gently, utilizing all the seven potentials or aspects of the God Self within: (1) the will, (2) the intelligence, (3) the love, (4) the cohesive force of crystallization and materialization, (5) the uni-fying and integrating substances of all, (6) the transmuting qual-ity, and (7) the rest and the peace upon that product created. Those are the seven aspects of Divine Energy in form, and in man as a son of or a co-creator with that divine activity.

While we contemplate all these attributes, talents, functions, re-sponsibilities of man as a child of this Energy, we must recognize that none of it is his to create or to bring about out of his own self-will, out of his own self-knowledge, out of his own self-love and out of his own self-recognition, because we understand that he is part of Divine Mind and the Force that creates him in the first place.

## RELATIONSHIPS OF REALMS

But now we come to the relationship of man to the angelic, the devic and the elemental forces as they relate to his functioning on the Earth planet itself. With the creation of a physical body and the ability to think through that physical realm and body, we know that we utilize the various elements of the planet itself on which

67

we have created this body and this form. But we also recognize that this is not the whole, the total or the essence of the individual who has done the creating. That is the spiritual Self, and the form is but a creation of that spiritual Self.

The elements, then, are not part of man's creative ability but are utilized by man in order to create a form through which he can express this desire, this thought and this energy, utilizing the laws of which he himself is a part. The total sum of these elements, in their various relationships to the species that are involved and which sustain the life form man has created for himself, are called the devic elemental forces.

For they comprise the various elements in their different functions and in their graduating, externalized forms; which become independent of the thought, the contemplation, the understanding and the respect man has shed upon them and which he shares in his experience upon that particular planet or plane where he is going through externalization himself, and an evolutionary process along with it. Thus man utilizes every single form or devic development that works in and through that congregated conglomerate of action as projected out from pure thought and energy.

In order to keep these devic processes balanced, interrelating and manageable, we of the angelic realm supersede, conduct, govern and work with and through their evolution as a process of creation. It is similar to any hierarchal workings or setup where you have the governing principles involved. The people make up the government. The local area, which is specific and individual, has its councilmen and mayors, you might say. Above those you have a national or international interest of governors, presidents, senators, dictators, or what you will call them. Even supreme above all this are the archangels, seven in number, who govern all these elements and all these devic developments wherever they might be in this solar system, galaxy and universe in which you are involved as a son of God evolving throughout all time and all space.

## MAN'S STATUS

This comprehension is certainly more than you even can begin to discern in your present consciousness. But because you are more than the present consciousness—which we are addressing in the Son light of your beingness, a child of God and a part of that Divine Mind and Energy in action—we know we speak to that part which remembers, which works with and can control all of these elements, congregations or devic developments, and can come into a

68

proper relationship with the angelic forces which help to keep all things balanced and in orbital relationship harmoniously and undisturbed, one with the other.

That is your function, to know these functions of ours, as well as it is for us to know yours and to step out of the way where we can and to help you to comprehend your function and possibilities properly, without grading them down or harming them in any way whatsoever that would destroy the equilibrium of all life force in its balance with one another and to the general well-being of each other.

With these understandings we can address the more complex conditions and bring you to a divine purpose of your present status and unfolding, without actually disturbing the equilibrium you have balanced delicately between the conscious, subconscious and superconscious memory patterns. All of these are most delicate. Each area is one that takes total concentration of the individualization or Sonship, God Self, within; your Christ identity, it is called.

Each one who can comprehend these things has come to know, and to have rapport with, his own individual spiritual Christ consciousness. Otherwise these words, these contacts and these communications would have no meaning and no value for you at this present time. So, should you fall into that category, know that you have much more to do on the workings-out within yourself of the awareness of your specialization or specific relationship to the Godhead.

It is not that we condemn or exclude you. It is that we clarify and try to aid you in your own ongoing processes within. We encourage and we teach, also we help you to discern, that status and area where you need to have further unfoldment from within your own beingness as a son of God and a child of the light which works with that energy, that light, through the love process.

## EXAMINATION OF THOUGHT FORMS

These thought forms you have created and are creating are extremely important for you to know about and to work with consciously. For there are thought forms you have created that must be dissolved in the coming New Age of Aquarius that befalls you shortly and toward which you are evolving and growing in every single step of the way you work and seek further illumination.

My intention here is to bring to your attention the fact that these thought forms are so important to your conscious comprehension at this time, that you examine every thought that exists, whether it has form in a specific frequency of life energy physically, as we call a species or part of life on the Earth, or whether it has only a concept unfolding and working out in the Earth pattern as you now know it.

So many concepts that are working in the Earth planet at this time through the race of man are unnecessary and are stumbling blocks to his own growth and further pattern of spiritual development. Therefore, it is your responsibility to work with those thought forms via the mathematical formulas and the scientific principles we have laid out here and have given you to understand, but only in part; because of your spiritual intuitions from within that you can do this now and must do this as a concerted action of the hundred and forty-four thousand light workers forming a new body, a new intention and a new purpose to the evolutionary grace and the gradual growth of mankind in the Earth and throughout this present solar system.

As far as you know, you have only this Earth with which to work. We have told you and have informed you that the astral planes are very much involved with the development of this Earth. But you cannot control the astral, you can only be aware of it, connect with it and concern yourselves with its process and progress as much as you are concerned with that of the Earth where you are presently incarnated at this time.

## UNIFIED ACTION

Incidentally, in recording these interviews we speak as emphatically and as specifically to those who are on the astral as we do to those who are on the Earth, for this information goes forth and broadcasts itself into every area below the angelic, celestial realm. So, this includes not only the astral but all the light forces who are in the ascended realms of the etheric vibration of our solar system. But since you are concerned only with the Earth and not with the astral, not with the etheric, and certainly not with the other planets in this solar system, you must begin to work where you are and through the area of contact where you are; which is the Earth planet, physically speaking, now.

By the fact that we have mentioned that a hundred and forty-four thousand light workers must come into a concerted, unified action together, we imply there is much work to be done, there are many contacts to be made, there is much spreading of the news and the information that come forth through these messages via this channel and the unit known as Mark-Age, which has the responsibility to record, to broadcast and to publish all of this for the New Age of Aquarius coming up.

You see that the work begins in small, minute manners in individual ways, and then grows and expands in a proper sequential order that is divinely led but is cooperatively, coordinately consigned with man as an individual and as a spiritual, conscious function where, in the personality aspect, he is contacting his own Christ Self and fulfilling that of his own Christ identity or cosmic energy source.

In all these things we speak to specific individuals. In all these things we speak to the entire race of man. In all these things we give homage and thanks to the Creater Who is, the idea that came from the source, the light that activated that source, and the Sonship through which we all are participating. Since all are parts of God and creations of that God Force, therefore we all consider ourselves as sons or children of that Light, that life, as love. Amen.

I am Jophiel of the Second Ray, speaking through the mind of the channel who is known as Yolanda of the Sun, in conjunction with her Nada consciousness or Self, which is part of the divinity in the race of man. Amen.

# 7. LOVE AND CREATION

## INDIVIDUALIZATION THROUGH LOVE

Chamuel speaks for the third aspect of God's activity, which is individualization through love. These steps or procedures, which bring about your own forms and future progresses, are related to the divine laws which operate throughout all kingdoms, for all areas of expressions, and for the entire evolutionary pattern which permits such. You are not to try to precipitate matter in your own plan and configurations but are to follow the divine workings-out or purposes.

This is where error has crept in and that is why I have had to replace that one called Lucifer, the fallen star and the archangel who had been in charge, until his descent into matter, of this individualization love aspect. You will be given a clarification of this when I am ready to speak of it. Before that you must come to see how love of the two preceding aspects or the duality of the Father-Mother God precipitates the third, which is love, the feeling, the desire for form or specific innovation.

In the realms of angelic responsibilities and activities I am preceding all specific form, which comes under the Fourth Ray or the fourth aspect of life. As you have been told, this form takes on many, many aspects and not singularly that which you call third dimensional material form, as that is one of the lowest outpourings of the spirit in activity; and one of the shortest-range aspects, as you have come to understand.

Several million years or a billion years in time preparing a form, expressing in a form and then dissolving a form, each one taking millions and billions of years as you understand it, is as nothing in the fourth expression of this adventure we call Divine Energy in contemplation of Itself, loving Its parts enough to create individualizations of It, and then from this triune aspect developing the fourth or the foundation upon which to build a form.

72

Remember too that each one of these steps, energies, expressions of Spirit has within it mathematical formulas and actual substance beyond that which you understand in the term of *substance*. These are, as we have said, thought forms or energies in operation. Those of the angelic kingdom supervise these exact expressions as they are fragmented from the divine whole.

So, those in the Third Ray or flame, the trinity aspect, over which I am in charge, are particularly concerned with those energy frequencies, vibratory rates, formulas which express the spark of love, desire, feeling coming from Divine Mother, Divine Father activities. Life, light and love, this is your divine trinity. From this comes form.

## AREAS OF EVOLVEMENT

In the formulation of this you may express in many myriad ways. That also is to be explained mathematically here. In every aspect you have a triune principle, which is symbolized by the downward pointing of your triangle. Superimposed over that and interpenetrating it is the next triune principle or activity.

In this solar system, therefore, we have four such triangular aspects or areas of evolvement and development. Your third dimensional plane, or what we call the Earth planet, expresses the first, as far as you are concerned; looking from this level, going up into evolution, rather than looking from the divinity or the outward expression and the eventual destiny, down into material matter or third dimensional frequency plane of your life.

You express on three levels of consciousness. These are the three planes of thinking: conscious, subconscious and superconscious. It is naturally the superconscious area which creates the conscious mind and controls the subconscious recordings of your past experiences. The point of the triangle imbedded in the Earth planet, let us say, is your point of expression or your physical body through which these three aspects or planes of consciousness are energizing.

The point of the higher realm, beyond which you have physical expression, is your fourth dimensional body as expressed through the full Christ consciousness and powers. This is what we have called your fourth dimensional light body or resurrected form. It interpenetrates sufficiently into your superconscious awareness that you may become evidential to the third dimensional frequency plane or the Earth planet, just as Jesus the Christ demonstrated in

73

his seven initiations upon the Earth planet, all during his incarnations as Sananda, the Christ or Prince of this plane and planet.

Above and beyond this dimension of Earth you have two subsequent areas of triangulations. In other words, there are seven planes above this through which you can express in what is now termed the astral, going into the etheric. These are not what you suppose them to be. They are areas or planes of consciousness, plus dimensions upon which to express those planes of consciousness, where you can evolve sufficiently and solidify your higher aspects or your Sonship, correspond to your subconscious records and experiences outside of this plane or planet known as the Earth dimension, and balance out whatever effects you have caused from your areas of thought, feeling and activity.

## PLANES OF CONSCIOUSNESS

Again we speak to you of these three planes of consciousness which are your divine heritage and your divine expression. You are part of this triune aspect of God, Which is mind, thought, love. The mind of God in you has the idea or the original word or purpose for being. The feminine aspect—which is thought or contemplation, the workings-out and the activities of that idea—is infused with the love of all of this and therefore creates an outer expression, whether it be a concept, a way of life or an actual physical phenomenon. Those physical phenomena could be a form or a body, as we already have indicated, or they can be the workings-out of an expression within you creatively, an ideology, a governmental structure, a religious experience.

All of these are terms which will mean something to you in your present evolutionary pattern, but are not the total or sublime aspect or way of expressing these energies within your consciousness. For you go on much beyond this plane of existence and you have a much higher way of expressing these so-called activities of man.

Beyond the areas we term for you as astral are the three planes above this called the etheric, shared by all in this particular solar system. They are the tenth, the eleventh and the twelfth planes of consciousness, which are the expressions of your higher Self, your Christ identity, fully manifested. You will note again the mathematical formula here. Ten, eleven and twelve are one, two and three. As in the beginning, so in the end. There is no beginning and there is no end.

However, as we have indicated to you, there is an overlapping process between each of these areas—Earth, astral and etheric—so that on the Earth you have the potential of four planes of activity, on the astral you have a potential of eleven areas of activity, on the etheric you have the potential of four levels of activity, making it complete.

The interpenetrating prospect is to give you a transitional period of trial and error, and a magnetic pull toward the next higher goal. You are never left in an area of expression longer than you need to be. You are always attracted, through the magnetic qualities of your own development, to the proper place. But it is the angelic kingdoms which provide you with the thought energy and the form for you to go into or to step into that next area comfortably.

## PLANES, PLANETS, DIMENSIONS

We speak here of planes, planets and dimensions. Let us try to clarify what we are expressing, now that we have given you some of the proper procedures by which you may express your divinity Self. A plane is an area of consciousness. A planet is a fully manifested congregation of individuals who are endeavoring and striving to express the same and to share the same, to coordinate the same, planes of consciousness. A dimension is an experience or a way of expressing this particular energy thought pattern and contemplation of your consciousness.

You can be expressing a fourth dimensional concept or energy in a third dimensional plane or planet such as the Earth; which is your resurrected body. But you are not sharing that with a great number of others, for you have broken the mold of that particular area or you are introducing the next higher step or plane of consciousness; which is the fourth dimensional plane of consciousness, in this case. This is what Jesus exacted for you and prepared for you, and expects of you in this present time and era you are stepping into from the Piscean Age into the Mark Age into the Aquarian Age.

The Mark Age, in this instance, is that transitory period when you break the mold as a group and help to dissolve that third dimensional plane of consciousness, and all the planetary structure that has adhered itself to that plane or that dimension of expression, so you collectively may dissolve what has been in operation for many millions of years as far as the race of man is concerned, and many billions of years as far as the planetary structure or logos is concerned. This is not destructive. This is transmuting, elevating, and evolutionarily wise and necessary.

75

As you step up into the astral expressions you are capable of expressing the fourth dimensional frequency body and may pass through those planes swiftly or slowly, according to what you have experienced elsewhere and what you have cleansed in the process of your going from third into fourth dimensional frequency body. But you must pass through that plane entirely.

There are seven planes of consciousness in the astral, seven levels upon which you may express. These are reflected also into the Earth consciousness as a mirror into your subconscious mind, into your conscious mind and into your superconscious mind or plane of consciousness. But in the astral you must pass through those seven planes.

When you are in the sixth and the seventh planes of the astral you already are expressing through your etheric body or your higher, spiritual Self and can move very quickly into the tenth, the eleventh and the twelfth spheres of expression. Beyond this is the celestial plane. This superimposes over all throughout this galaxy. Since you are concerned through this time and place only with what is concerned for your solar system, we will not penetrate the areas beyond this expression.

But you must come to understand that there are a normal development and progression of ideas and series of steps that must be taken, for there is no breaking the continuity in anyone's evolvement or development as a child of God through this solar system. So it was created from the heights and descended into matter or physical life form. But we have taken you up from the place where you are, in order to prepare you for the places that have been made ready for your ascent out of matter and back into your divine heritage and proper structure as a son of God.

In these planes and planets of expression are many of your sisters and brothers of Christhood and of the race of man expressing and experiencing life and form as you know it. We say *as you know it,* for their lives are developed according to congregations and segments of attraction. They are in congregations or planetary structures that can best befit and hold their interests in order to learn and to grow from where they are in the plane of consciousness and in the dimension of expression which best suits their evolutionary progress.

These are part of your own species. These are part of your own background. These are relatives, in a sense. Some of you have been associated with these various individualizations of God in one form or another, be it on Earth, the astral, the etheric or in one of the planes or the planets surrounding you and evolving beyond you in the present.

## AREAS FOR EXPERIENCING

Remember too that often as you go from life expression into another life expression, since there is no such thing as death of your soul and mind and spirit, you may experience a form other than what relates to Earth plane living. You may go far beyond the third dimensional frequency form, after a transition from that area of expression, into an eighth, a ninth, a tenth or an eleventh plane of expression. This may involve other planets, or it may involve just a plane of consciousness where you remain suspended, learn, grow, follow the record of your past, and determine to speak up again and to take upon yourselves the responsibility of another experience or expression of your God Self.

In other words, since you have three planes of consciousness in and through all areas of existence—which in this area of time we call conscious, subconscious and superconscious expression—you have that same faculty and can live in or express through any one of those three areas or planes of consciousness at any one time.

If you are suspended between experiences and dwell only in the subconscious realm or plane of life in order to review and to cleanse what has gone before, you can remain inanimate for a time; or, as you would put it on Earth, asleep for a time.

If you wish conscious expression which coincides with a physical form in order to engage actively in experience and matter in that area you have become magnetically attracted to via your past and future goals, you may proceed into that. But if you are ready to deal with your superconscious activities only and to remain in that plane of activity without formulating or expressing outwardly, in a rest state, you may absorb many new talents, ideas and learnings through that process.

Therefore, provided for your experience are these many areas or dimensions for activity. In those dimensions we have created form through our angelic realms of responsibility. From out of your thought patterns, your thought desires and your spiritual activities and realizations, we of the angelic realm can create a form upon which you as a son of God may experience and express. These are the planes, planets and dimensions of this solar system and beyond. They also include the physical form, as you call physical, through

77

which you express these aspects of your consciousness, of your awareness, of your activities and of your desires.

## FALL WITH LUCIFERIAN FORCES

When the desire is altruistic there are no problems in your evolutionary pattern and progress. When they are unselfish or to be returned unto the cosmic pattern of creation, they require little or no supervision, for you are in the divine grace and the grip of your own spirituality and creative seed of knowledge. But when you recognize this power, this knowledge and this activity and erroneously proceed to disassociate it with the divine head or Source, you become misinformed, mismanaged and filled with the mischief of your own creative ideas, purposes and plans. This is how the Luciferian forces fell into matter.

For the original and only sin of all is self-aggrandisement, self-purpose; or selfishness, as you call it. To think of the self-power, the self-purpose of the individualization of these creative principles then requires a series of steps and experiences that allows you to reevaluate that toward which you erroneously have pointed yourselves.

In this manner has man been entrapped with the Luciferian forces on the Earth plane and planet. For the purpose and the thoughts and the activities have been of a selfish nature. The thoughts emanating out of all these formulations created by your desire, your feelings, your motives, your plans, and not the spiritual evolutionary ones, have congealed and have made into the Earth planet and plane an entire world of selfishness. We use this term very loosely and all-encompassing for the very activities to which we refer.

## BALANCING OF IMBALANCES

The higher Self, the spiritual goals and missions of any force are those that speak of equal sharing, equal opportunities, equitable arrangements of all that exists for the good of all who are expressing in the same area of development. In the broadest sense this does include every life form and every element.

But when one superimposes over another or shares only an insignificant amount of his bounty with another, you have much imbalance in the area of expression, mentally, emotionally and spiritually speaking. These imbalances then create other imbalances. Until you bring about a balance on Earth in these things,

78

you never can create a truly spiritualized energy comparison and bring the entire species of man, with his brethren of the other dimensions and the other kingdoms elsewhere, into a profitable and sharing arrangement which will enhance all equally and will develop all simultaneously.

That must be the purpose of any dimension of activity. It must be the purpose of any planet that is expressing anywhere, because when the imbalances occur, the thought patterns circulating then create all kinds of upheavals and catastrophies. This is not to say that there are not upheavals and imbalances elsewhere, but there are none so inequitable and so catastrophic as those we have upon the Earth plane and planet at this present time.

Naturally, the upheavals you are going through in the Mark Age or transitory period between the Piscean and the Aquarian Ages are amongst the most horrendous that ever have been on the planet during its entire evolutionary periods, because you are bringing all imbalances back into an equitable sharing of life forms expressing normally and naturally to their fullest expression with their fullest intent from the original purpose of their being. This includes all the elements, all the life forms and man himself.

## REEVALUATION FOR PROGRESSION

So, you will see rare occasions occurring on the Earth in these end days, as you call them, because total concepts, thought forms, energy patterns will be torn from their original orbit or purpose or plane of activity and will be returned unto the source of their being for reevaluation and a new opportunity to express elsewhere. This does include the race of man at this particular time as he is expressing in a form upon the Earth dimension, or the foursquare form of Earth plane life as you know it. In this respect let us look closely at what we mean here.

Man's spiritual consciousness and awareness are now introducing in the planet those higher motives and those original purposes for which he was created. Therefore, the Luciferian forces, which exist only by the thought patterns and are fed by additional thought patterns, are at war with one another. They are at grips with the influencing powers that dominate the plane of activity you call Earth. Man in his coming spiritual awareness, which has taken thousands of years to solidify and to anchor through on this plane and planet, is now destroying or nullifying that which has held him in total persuasion for two hundred and six thousand years.

You must recognize that this is not a sudden, erratic or impetuous thing which is occurring. It is the result of much mismanagement; but normal procedure in the divine way of working out energy, form, thought, love and desire. These four aspects must come into their proper mathematical formula in order to restate, to reconstruct, that which is for the ongoing and evolutionary process of all spiritual structures. It never has been concluded that that which is in power, rightly or wrongly, can remain so, for all things move and have being in energy and in thought. So, therefore, they re-evaluate, re-form and reorganize themselves.

## RELATIONSHIP WITH ANGELIC KINGDOM

That our function in the celestial planes is to provide a form through which these reevaluations take place is but an interrelationship, or of interest, to you as the race of man, the sons of God, but is not your responsibility. For we will re-form all your thoughts, energies and planes of consciousness and will help to provide you with a form through which you may express, provided you make that freewill choice.

This is the conscious aspect of the triune part of mankind, aided by his superconscious. Through the subconscious aspect or plane of activity in his eternalness, he and the angelic realms create the suitable form through which the conscious, superconscious and subconscious activities or planes of awareness are able to express outwardly and to secure anchor, and to congregate with equals and associates, or what we call individualizations, of that same divinity which are in the same species and correlating species.

Man ever must learn to cooperate with, to coordinate with and to plan with, consciously and superconsciously through his subconscious memory track, others of his own kind and with others who are not of his kind so that there is ever an interrelating cooperative ongoing, an experience, with all other species and forms; or kingdoms, as we often term them. So, man must know his relationship with the angelic realm, and man must know his relationship with all the other forms of life in the area or dimension where he finds himself needing an expression in form.

That we have interrelating aspects and cooperative functions together is part of the expansion of consciousness and awareness as a son of God and a part of this great divine plan and activity. Therefore, the combinations are endless, as you can see, of what man can experience within himself, with others of his own kind, with lower and higher creations and forms.

80

## RELATIONSHIP WITH LUCIFERIAN FORCES

So must he learn his relationship with the Luciferian forces, which he has helped to strengthen in his own way. For as man fell into matter and was attracted to the form and the area that were provided by those angelic individuals who wished to experience their powers of and for their own selfish motives, man became a partner with, and then became enslaved by, the higher energy forms that were created.

Let us look at this selfishness—or sin, as it is often called—in its true light and perspective. It is merely the negation of that which is true and just. It is deliberate disassociation with the highest within him; seeking the self-expression or falling in love with the power that was placed there from beyond his own creative ability.

As we have said over and over again: man cannot create, he can only co-create. Man is not the originator, or the creation itself is not the originator, and never can be the originator. This applies to the angelic kingdoms as well as to the race of man and to all other species. But when man or the angelic force recognizes this tremendous power and creative force within himself, and falls in love with it because it does exist in him, he turns away from the originator and sees himself. It is narcissism, in a sense. For how can you love more that which is in you than that Which put it there in the first place?

This is the fault, this is the error. And error compounds error when it refuses to see truth. Therefore, these errors have been compounded. These errors have created form, for the angelic kingdom is capable of creating form in order to house its ideas and its responsibilities and thoughts that emanate from out of that dimension or plane of activity. Man, guilty of the same, has fallen into the similar trap and then has become enmeshed in it with those forces which helped create the form in the first place.

This does not mean that all men have fallen into that trap, because there are areas and segments of the society of the race of man who never have fallen into that trap, just as there are angelic forces who never have fallen into that trap, of self-perpetuation, self-enjoyment, denying the Source of that self and seeing the self as higher than the Source; which is totally impossible and is destined for failure.

## REHABILITATION OF ERROR FORCES

No matter how long it takes, the destiny remains. We speak here in millions and billions of years, which are far beyond your mortal

81

comprehension, and even your superconscious aspects of recognizing them. But since the superconscious is that connection with the source and the seed of origination, you can reach for it and work with it and be comfortable in the concept of it.

But regardless of how much time it takes, the destiny is precluded. For all forces which turn away from the source of light, falling in love with their own powers that are ever with them and never can be withdrawn from them—for they are created of the one Source; and energy cannot be destroyed, it just can be re-formulated and remanipulated—the destiny of these sources and forces which are in error is to be recaptured, rehabilitated, resuscitated back into the light and the love of God, which are eternal.

We ask now how this can be done. It can only be done through the Third Ray aspect, which is love. Love, which is the key to all, is that which shall return the self-love into the selfless love from which it originally was created. Love must conquer in this respect, for it was in the area of love that the fall occurred. Love, then, must be the activity, in its proper and true light, that rehabilitates that which erred in the first place.

Does this mean love of self or does it mean the love of spiritual Self? Naturally, it must be a doubled effort by those who are in the Earth and who come to recognize the reason for the fall into self and matter and error and sin, to bring about a higher form with renewed energy and with renewed expression, exercising all of the preceding planes of consciousness. Into this must we pour every available source and individualization. Therefore, the recruiting by those of the celestial and etheric forces in this solar system has gone beyond anything that ever before has occurred in the history of this solar system.

It is a one-time opportunity, as you might put it. It has been millions of years since the fall or the descent into matter by man, attracted by the selfishness, the self-love of the Luciferian angelic realm which created a form for man because of his desire to express for himself, to try evolution for himself, to flex his spiritual powers in his own way and for his own purposes and for his own selfish reasons.

He saw, he knew, he felt the powers of the spirit within him and decided to experience them for himself and for his own advantages, particularly in the areas of dominating and controlling other life forms which became enslaved to him. So, he who would enslave became enslaved. Man, who was attracted to this area because of the opportunities to conquer, to express and to show power

82

over other and lesser forms, became entrapped by the very form he helped create or helped inaugurate.

This is why your prophets and teachers, such as Jesus, have said, "Ye are the sons of darkness, you are the sons of Satan," meaning the nature or the ideas of these Luciferian errors are those which you wish to perpetuate yourselves. We speak here, of course, of those who still seek power over others, domination over other forms of life; and the noncaring in the use of the other elements of the planet upon which man lives as a temporary abode and a hospitality house for his physical body and form.

## SHARING

You cannot go on abusing and misusing, and not caring about, that which you share. You must have as much concern for it and those parts of it as you have for every single part of your own body and your own consciousness. You may not continue to push aside the higher thoughts within yourself—the conscience, as some put it—and say: that does not matter, that cannot do me any harm, I am in power over all things.

For you are not. You must share, and share alike. You must be responsible for and love all equally to that which you love most dearly in yourself. What is it that man, or any life form, loves most dearly within himself, but the Life Source Itself? Living, thinking, feeling; this is life and energy, or God within you, expressing outwardly, that you love, that you cherish, and that you must love and cherish in all other things as much as you do in yourself.

When you can share this equally and care about it equally for all other forms of life as you care about it for yourself, you will rehabilitate all other forms of life and will free the Luciferian forces from their own error ways. These angelic forces which have created a form through which you can express these error concepts then can be freed from themselves. For they are the agents of, and the forces which follow, the thought patterns created by the race of man in order to give him form and place to express.

## NEXT THREE THOUSAND YEARS

That is why your responsibility is doubled in this time of *now*. We speak of the time and say it cannot be done in the interim period which we term the Mark Age period of time. For this is the period of time of cleansing, reevaluating and reconstituting those

83

thought forms which are going to have power and energy from the race of man for the next ensuing era of time called the Aquarian Age.

In other words, in the next two thousand years of time you will bring about these renewed energies, these renewed forms, these renewed opportunities which have been in congregation and orbit for this plane and planet or dimension as it now expresses through you and with you and for you to experience upon.

That is but a brief outline of how the Third Ray or the love aspect has worked, does work and will work for you and with you. I am Chamuel, in charge of this aspect throughout the universe as you may come to know it, in time. Particularly in the next three thousand years of time, as man will express in the solar system, he will have opportunity to come to know all of the universe and all of the powers, the forces, the sources and the forms which express in and throughout this universe. But for the present time we give you this type of an outline.

The thousand years of time for man to experience on the Earth in the incoming Age of Aquarius will give him the opportunity to anchor and to solidify totally the fourth dimensional consciousness and form upon the Earth. In other words, he will dissolve, in that thousand-year period of time, all the third dimensional frequency form as he now experiences and knows it. This will be the total concentration of all etheric masters and all sons of God related to the Earth planet and its evolvement in the past two hundred and six million years.

For the next two-thousand-year period of time man will come to know and to conquer his entire solar system and to govern it justly and rightly so it too can go on into its next period of evolution and can exchange with all life forms, sources and opportunities as we have outlined to you here in the four triangulated areas and planes of development.

There are thirteen planes which he will come to know about; with the thirteenth, of course, going outside of this solar system and universe. In the next three-thousand-year period of time man will be able to contemplate and to appreciate, and to come into conscious contact with, this thirteenth plane, or outside of his solar-system range.

So be it in truth. Through love I give this decree and announcement. Through love I prepare this formulation of your thoughts. As you can see, the long-range prospects are greater than you can contemplate in one lifetime, or even in your own superconscious plane of activity. Amen. Chamuel, Chamuel, Chamuel: in this is the key and the code. For in all occult activity and knowledge are known the trade secrets of the name of love in this time.

*Sons of the light, arise.*
*Sons of the light, love.*
*Sons of the light,* be.

# 8. LOVE RADIATION

## CONTEMPLATION

We continue now to explore avenues of love radiation, or the feeling nature, as one of the most essential triune principles in creative life form. As we go from this concept into our higher realms of expression, I, Chamuel, will guide you in thinking about contemplation and in preparing you for the truest manifestation of frequency form wherever it may evolve and develop, projected by, heralded by, prepared by the Gabriel angelic forces.

All of this is simple, practical and fundamental to everything you will discern and will be able to co-create with your higher spiritual powers. But it is agreed that it takes a great deal of studying and analyzing from the intellectual point of view, because you have fallen from the grace of your Christ consciousness in this area of development for so many eons of time that we are required to work slowly and methodically in this particular manner in order to bring you back up out of the intellectual, analyzing, reasoning, rationalizing mind; which has become the most predominant factor in your entire existence, through the brain development of the physical man, in part, on Earth.

## SEVEN DIVINE STEPS OR ASPECTS

But let us backtrack for a few moments and be resolved unto the meaning of much of spiritual application that thus far has been given to you in these discourses through the archangels, and my particular function as channeling the love radiations from the Divine Mind and the divine activity, Father-Mother God, into the third aspect, which is love and the area or the triune part which creates the Son and all creative, manifested form.

Before time began—which is merely a way of marking easy developmental processes of growth and evolution of that which is created by Divine Mind and divine activity, Father-Mother God—we see the two dual aspects fused to become what you might call friction energy, the molecular thought form; for want of a better term, called love. This is the divine feeling nature that brings about a so-called fourth step or need, that need being form.

From this step we go into that which must integrate all forms or unify them and put them in their proper, respective places and relationships, keeping them balanced or whole, as they all derive from the same Source and have within them the same properties and aspects, the trinity relationship; and go from there into the sixth step of refinement, purification and spiritual transmutation. Transmutation is one of the most important aspects of all activity, since Source or Divine Mind and divine activity can never remain stationary or still. It must keep aspects of Itself gradually evolving and dissolving and remanifesting into form, for this is the nature of Divine Energy and love.

But the seventh step or the final step is the completion of all the previous steps, and marks the end of such activity. Therefore, it relates back to the first step or idea, having gone through all other aspects of God in action. Therefore, the seventh step or the ray of divinity in its purification and completion is returned unto its source or idea; but is never the same, because it has gone through the various six preceding steps and therefore incorporates all the six aspects of God within itself and completes itself. That is why there is no beginning and there is no end. And it is only in Divine Mind that we can even subdivide the one, the whole, the all, Which is God, to begin with.

So, if we look at the mathematical formulas we see that the one unified God, Which is all that there is, is indivisible. Yet, within that indivisibility there are seven steps or aspects that can be conceived of by reasoning, intellectual, and even spiritual, mind consciousness. But God is not dual or two. There is no personification of a Father and a Mother God, except that this is the best terminology we can give when relating to those things that appear or exist or are working themselves out on the plane of action where you are.

Therefore, when you pick up a solid form and see it as a whole, you still can see two sides of it. Yet, it is not divided in itself, it is whole. Such is the nature of God energy, life force, light and creation. All of creation together is one, as part of the One; and undivided in this respect, for God sees no division in Himself or in His creations. Because of this love of and understanding of all that is, we return the love aspect, which is the most powerful part of Self-contemplation, and see it in the completion, the wholeness, the fulfillment and the resting aspect, which we call the peace and the love of God, for God and in God of the Seventh Ray aspect.

## CHOICE OF RIGHT OR WRONG

In this respect the Third Ray function or concept is the same as the Seventh. In this way the Seventh incorporates all the other six. But in the process of reaching this Seventh Ray aspect of completeness and wholeness, and at the end returning to the beginning, the alpha and the omega, we have the choice at the third step or in the Third Ray contemplation and activity; which results in the downfall if the wrong choice is made.

But not all are in that category, and everyone must not submit himself to the crucible through which this energy and activity take place. For in the inanimate object world and in the lower forms of life upon the kingdom called Earth you have not seen that Third Ray aspect come to pass.

Except for the race of man, who governs and rules the planet upon which he now resides in this era and age, along with those angelic forces that created a form through which he might express this negativity or denial of his true nature and being, we have not been subjected to the process as necessary now for the Mark Age period of time or the cleansing, purification of the Sixth Ray of transmutation, in order to reach the Seventh Ray or step of returning unto the Source, Which is God, totalness, oneness, unity and wholeness. You have in each of these aspects and steps a period of time in which to choose right from wrong. The longer you delay the process the longer it takes to reach the ultimate goal; which is, from the Seventh Ray returning unto the First Ray or aspect.

## MICHAEL AS SOLAR LEADER

In that respect you have Michael, head of the angelic forces of the First Ray and titular head of all archangels throughout our solar system with which we are concerned. Michael, then, has become, and must take this responsibility as, the titular head of this particular solar system until the race of man is totally unified and brought into his fullness and completion of all the seven ray aspects on Earth and through all planes, planets, dimensions and faculties. You have known this for a period of time through the dictations submitted to and through this channel and we will not belabor the point at this time.

Furthermore, it has been given that when all the sons of God on the Earth and through the solar system reach the proper place of elevation and evolution, powers and expressions of their Sonship with God, you will have Lord Michael, or Katoomi as he is called on the Hierarchal Board, removed from this solar system as the titular head of the Hierarchal Board or governing body of the sons of God on this planet and solar system.

But until that time, which is the long period and process we have tried to outline for you herewith as regards the solar system history of the next three thousand years of time, we are aiding and assisting Lord Michael, through our realms and roles as archangels in charge of all angelic form, all devic and elemental form, in this solar system and beyond, to complete that which must be done due to the original fall of man and the Archangel Lucifer in this particular solar system.

## MANIFESTATION OF FORM

As we have indicated, it is necessary first to have the desire of form in matter before the archangels and the angelic kingdoms, the devic forces, and the elements that comprise the devas can proceed to make ready a suitable house or vehicle on which to express.

Out of this divine action and idea which we term the Father-Mother God in total balance, harmony and equality, we see set in motion concepts or projections of ways and means to share, to express, to be concerned with, regimentation or law; the law here being the ability to express this divinity in balance, positive and negative polarities, in the infinite variety of manners that are possible. It becomes again a mathematical exercise that is infinite in number and variety. For no two thoughts, ideas and actions combined with the love aspect that is caused by this activity and idea combined can ever be duplicated and can ever be completed, in as far as frequency of number is concerned.

But the areas upon which this can occur also are very diverse and complicated. In other words, depending on how much quality and quantity of thought contemplation, energy and force are put into the activity of such balanced equations, we have the degree or the quality of its manifested form. This is the job and the function of the angelic kingdom, and is certainly not a potential or a problem to be concerned with and worked out by the mortal mind or by the spiritual consciousness of the sons of God.

For theirs is to govern justly, rightly and harmoniously that which has been created in those areas where they are permitted incarnation, expression and adventure for their own expansion, for their own interest and for their own Self-realization of where they are, who they are and what their potentials must be.

## KINGDOMS OR PLANES OF ACTION

You must then resolve yourself to be confined to that area where you are able to do the most good and to be the most perfected in your own concept and purpose of being. But let us not digress too long in that respect, for we come back to the areas of evolvement and development that are yours to contemplate and to work with. We step forth into the first plane of action, which in your world is matter or form of the most fundamental nature. This is the mineral kingdom.

The second plane of action is that of the vegetable kingdom, which has within it an intelligence to expand and to grow in multiple ways not conceivable to or possible through the elemental kingdom that operates in the first plane of action, or the mineral kingdom. Therefore, you have hybrids and varieties of many unique kinds, ad infinitum, to that particular area or kingdom.

But when we come to the animal kingdom, of which man has made himself a part—but not purposely, because he never was supposed to be a part of the animal kingdom—we have a self-realization of continuity and the aspect of the third phrase or phase of Creative Force: God in action; which is love, feeling, desire. This is not equated to the first or the second planes of action, which are the mineral and the vegetable kingdoms. But in the third plane of action on the Earth you have this, and that is why it is called the third dimensional form.

In man as the son of God, with the Self-consciousness of his identity and the potential of his powers—which is the fourth dimensional frequency introduced into the third dimensional form which is the animal body—we have the Self-realization or the total completion of the fourth dimensional aspect of God, or the dual, negative-positive polarities, in its creation.

## DOUBLE DUALITY OF MAN

Let us review this simply. Four is the fundamental principle upon which all matter is built and all form is made complete. It is possible because it comprises a double duality: the duality of the Father-Mother God, positive and negative polarity, which is one

God Force in action; and the duality of the creation of the Mother-Father God, which is the Son, or all forms of creation; also an equalized polarity of positive and negative force within itself, and the ability through that form to realize its Maker or its Self-origin. This is the uniqueness of Christ consciousness or cosmic being in any plane of action where you may be confined or restored.

Simply, again, we say you who are the sons of God and born out of the Christ, cosmic consciousness must know and must realize that your form in nature, wherever you may be, is the result of a double duality, the duality of your God consciousness and the duality of the form where you are. You are the form of God in action. You are the creation of the Source, Creative Energy. But you must know yourself both as an identity of that creation and as the Creator Himself.

Where you fall afoul of your destiny and purpose is in that third aspect, or the trinity relationship as a Son form; knowing this power, knowing this potential, exercising these talents and utilizing them for the self-form in which you have found yourself.

Thus you become entrapped in it. You cut off yourself from the source of your supply and the source of your nourishment for ongoing, for development, for further creation. The long and arduous path back to this area of subsequent knowledge, subsequent expansion, subsequent infinite varieties of form and areas of exploration is in this restoration of your Self-contemplation.

## MAN AND LUCIFERIAN FORCES

We have given you information and indication that the inter-relationship between the sons of the Light and the Luciferian forces which created this form upon the Earth planet for exploration and extortion is both dual in nature and singular, in this respect: both occurred almost simultaneously in time and in development of the nature. In a sense, one might say it was and is one of the potentials of all life force to see, to know, to recognize, and to experiment with, this negation of itself.

But to say that God created evil or sin is a most ignorant and purposeless train of thought. For of course God consciousness or God activity has within it all potentials and possibilities. And among the highest aspects of Energy Force, life itself, is freedom to express, to explore, to grow. Therefore, all alternates to good are still possible because it is inherent.

Again we remind you of the single solid object that you pick up. It has many sides to it, yet it is unified and whole, and all sides of it

91

are indeed beautiful and part of that whole. What you do with it and how you use it is your own freewill choice. This must be inherent in all creation, for it is inherent in divine law and life and light, and is part of the love aspect as well.

When each of the creations of God could find the idea within itself to contemplate and to work with its own source of energy, which at best is temporary and short in relationship to the eternal evolution and expression of cosmic life and law and love, then that opportunity prevailed. So, the two became fused or related to one another out of the law of attraction. For you will be attracted to, and will draw unto you like a magnet, that which you contemplate and work upon.

So, as the sons of Light contemplated their own powers, lights, light force, energy, and dominion over all other lesser forms and those who were in the process of evolving to a higher expression, they attracted to themselves and were attracted by those of the angelic realm—or the Luciferian forces, as you might call them—who could create a form for them to express out of and to work through.

It is most difficult to say which preceded which in contemplation and thought, except to say that the two who were attracted and became one force, confined and imprisoned in one area of time, space and place which is the Earth, had fused because of this attraction of like mind, like interest and the like free will. The fact that the Luciferian forces were on the Third Ray or third aspect, of love, is the key to the hidden complexity or lock of this entire solar system and the race of man as he is evolving through this solar system.

## MIDAS PARABLE

You must then record the Midas aspect, as brought forth previously. It is from the legend, the memory, the conscious acceptance that those who become attracted to the power of the highest in themselves are trapped or cut off from their own source of supply. So, in speaking of these divine laws, and knowledge of truth as it has enfolded throughout the history of this solar system and particularly this planet, you were handed down a simile or parable that could be applicable to your everyday intimate life expression.

If you become so enamoured of that which you create and which can supply you with more of the same material goods you are enthralled with, eventually it chokes you to the point of death. For you are dead if you are not contemplating and aware of the Divine

Energy and true Self that exist within you, and your Source of life, light and love that is God and not yourself. For it was Midas who loved the gold he accumulated to such a degree that everything he touched, including his own food and substance, became that gold, and he was near to his death.

If, then, you take the second phase of that fable and understand that in order to release himself from this wish, desire or freewill choice which he made himself, out of his own power and glory and his ability to create—or to co-create, as the case may be, in the realm of man—we have the humor and the depth of sadness to know Midas' reward was his appearance as a fool. A fool, in this case, is symbolized by a donkey or an ass, which in symbology is to say a hybrid and not a pure, beautiful part of God which was originally intended to be.


## LOVE IN ACTION

In this aspect and in this relationship are we not all fools who see and know the truth, but act not with it and utilize it not and confine ourselves not to the divine which is within us, and be not content to choose that which is God and not that which is of man's own power? For man really has no power, nor have the angels, other than that which is given to them by the original Source and Creator, our Father-Mother God, the dual or equal polarities of positive and negative Energy in contemplation of Itself. We are but the third or trinity aspect of manifestation: love in action.

Now we complete this transmission and speak to you of the next to come, by Raphael, who shall teach you how to integrate and to unify yourselves with all souls, spirits, forms and creative principles in and through all eternity. Amen.

I am Chamuel, your blessed servant and agent of the Light; God-given to do this function, and to prepare His sons for theirs. I am honored and privileged to come through this channel in this way, and hope that all I have brought in love and divine truth shall serve you as it serves me and my angelic forces throughout all kingdoms concerning this universe. Amen.

I love God and, in loving Him Who is our Father-Mother Creator, love all that exists; for all that exists is the Father and Mother God. All that can be is in Him-Her; one, always and ever. Chamuel. Chamuel. Shemah, Israel, the Lord God is one.

# 9. INTEGRATION WITH ALL CREATION

## INTEGRATION PRINCIPLES

Raphael speaking. Those angelic forces of the Fifth Ray are integrating your consciousness, your experiences and your preparatory vibrational forces, to create form in whatever plane of action or dimension you may have existence. These integrating forces or principles are part of the very beginning of existence, never leaving, never separating, ever vigilant. They are inherent in the alpha and the omega of life itself.

It is code-contained in my name and responsibility. The *aelph* in Raphael is for this indication; as are the names and the codes of all higher beings, to give them the mathematical, as you term it, understanding and protection for their functions and jobs, and is part of your understanding now to comprehend this never-changing law. All are part of the code and integrated in the One, Which is God.

As soon as we have the dual aspects of God consciousness in operation—negative and positive polarity; or Mother-Father God, as you term it for now—we have the integrating or balancing faculties in immediate operation. For the two are one, and the one operates as seemingly two. Likewise, the third aspect of the Trinity, the Sonship or love emanating out of this dual operation and faculty, is one in it, part of it and totally balanced with it.

I am not aware of any place or time, any dimension or experience, where the Trinity can be separated. Any time, anyplace, anywhere the separation takes place there is an imbalance, and the integrating forces or wholeness of God action are improperly exercised and not to be considered perfect, pure and the substance of love in action.

So, we know that those who are of this thinking and activity cannot be in the right place and doing the proper works. Our endeavors then are to exercise our force, our understanding, our love and our unity in purpose, to bring about such a balance as it is in the beginning and is throughout all time and existence unto the end, which is the beginning of all.

No end, no beginning, no separation. This is the principle upon which we work and are working and have been working and ever shall work for the good of the whole, in which we are one with you. This is part of our teaching and our major responsibility unto the race of man as he goes forth into the various areas of exploration and experimentation.

In order to perform this we must bring about certain forms that can be utilized by mankind in these levels of expression. We assist all other angelic forces in this process. But since we are in the beginning and in the end the same, we do not see our energies and our specific duties in any way separated from theirs, either.

## DUPLICITY OF PURPOSES

Man has a duplicity of purposes, and must come to integrate them in his own consciousness before he can be permitted full power and full control over those forces which we guide and guard him in, in the present time and place of his evolutionary growth, particularly as it is resolving in this planet, on through the astral, into the etheric and overriding all superstructures for this solar system.

He is not in command of them as yet anywhere in this solar system. But that is why we have come and that is why we have channeled through broadcasting this light and information to you who are prepared to see and to know and to integrate all force, energy, light and understanding where you are now in your present embodiment, and will carry it through to all other existences as you evolve, grow and take this information into other areas throughout eternity.

It is again this integrating principle by which we operate, the fact that we can teach and can demonstrate, and can prove to your benefit and ability to accept, that which we have presented here. In doing so we know you will carry it through to your eternal existence. For truth is, and once implanted in your conscious mind it carries and works for you everywhere, on through eternity.

It is here and now that we wish to transmute and to transplant our expressions and exercises of function into your conscious applications so that when the time comes for you to supervise them yourselves you will be sufficiently prepared. This duplicity of which I have spoken in this case refers to the fact that though you are

95

created in the divine sense with this knowledge, you are not carrying this responsibility at this time.

So, in recapturing or remembering that which you are created to do and to know from the beginning, you likewise will carry with you and will add unto you a new and higher function as you go forward and reinstate yourselves properly as the sons of God. Is this not the magnificent way an all-powerful, all-knowing and all-loving Father-Mother God would work? Rehabilitated and returned unto the consciousness of this oneness in which you are, you not only are given all that you had before but have added unto you new and higher realms and powers and gifts of that Divine Parent.

## INTEGRATION OF FUNCTIONS

Man, as he travels through the various areas of consciousness, must know all that is applicable and functioning in those levels of awareness. Then, as he can integrate them with what he has learned in the past and what he is expected to learn in the present, and has an inkling of what is to come forth in the future, he prepares for himself, and is aided by the angelic kingdoms in seeking, a vessel through which to work.

Not only is the vessel prepared by him and his co-creations in Spirit which are the angelic kingdoms, but the areas themselves must be created, supervised and integrated. This is what the Raphael forces teach and demonstrate, and prepare you to experience and to take over for yourselves in the long and distant future ahead.

That is what you were preparing to do when the Luciferian forces and the segment of the race of man fell deeply into matter and lost touch with the reality and the truth of the purpose for which they were functioning and working, and fell in love with their own power that they felt and their own aspects of Godly, Creative Energy consciousness.

The integrating of these faculties and functions is always extremely subtle, for they must remain balanced with all other forms, forces and purposes at the same time. For one must never become more strong or more self-interested than any other force or form that is in the preparatory stage. For each one feeds upon the other or relates to the other in a harmonious whole and balance for the good of the whole. This tricky and seemingly subtle scale of balance is so only to that mind or consciousness that cannot see the total good in the various elements feeding upon and balancing with one another for the varied and multiple purposes involved.

We must see at all times that each one is a unit or an integrated force within itself, independent and functioning for the purpose of expressing a part of the God Energy Force in motion. In this first instance, each in his own independent, unique, functioning way is separated from each other; but is not separated. In this type of thinking or balance or positive equation, again we bring you to mathematical comprehensions. We see that what is, is not; and what is not, must be.

## BALANCING OF FORCES

So, with these independent units, as we will call them, or elements, integrating them, balancing them and keeping them whole in this equation becomes, or seems to become, a complexity unto the uninitiated mind, the unprepared mind and the unwilling heart. Wherever there is a sense of separation or independence that does not take into consideration this balance, this wholeness, this oneness, then you will have the other areas of thinking or desire emulating it, such as superiority, domination and force, in the negative sense. That is where all mischief and problems arise.

But now we speak of the beginnings and of the trial-and-error of creating the various areas for this type of development. We see that with harmony and love and truth and the understanding of the equitable arrangements of Spirit in all parts of Its multiple ways of expressing, we can have this experience to a very glorified degree. Then man and all the other forms of life which are related to man are given wonders and marvels to know, to experience and to experiment with in this sense of unification, balance and interdependence upon one another. It is here that the areas are under the control of the Raphael forces. For we see that all balance may be supplied, and returned unto the Source from which it came.

We see that the time involved and required relates only to that which is sufficient to the total comprehension and experience. While the integrating thoughts and avenues of expression are functional and can be expanded profitably and enjoyably, they exist. When they are not, the time comes to dissolve or to transmute them in the sixth step, or through the transmuting rays of Zadkiel's forces. This must be understood and known also by you so you are prepared for the time when all energy, all forms, all places are to be eliminated for the next step or some higher goal, if that is possible.

In some cases, as we will have upon the Earth in the next immediate era of time, referring here to thirty to forty more years, you will have the disintegrating of many of these imbalanced forces that will not work harmoniously and will not unite with one another and will not keep the total balance, be drawn away through their own magnetic force within, which is Spirit, to those areas where they will learn some of these harsh lessons, since the stubbornness exists and the resolve not to cooperate remains.

But we are concerned here in preparing for you the knowledge and the experience of the higher aspects and the more positive potentials that can come while you are in this state of consciousness—one of cooperation, coordination, love and harmony—to be balanced with all who are in the same frame of reference and desire. It is ever necessary to rebalance these forces, for at all times there is this process going on of one dominating the other or one receiving more than the other at different times. Therefore, in keeping this equitable balance we are in operation and in consciousness of it at all times in the process of growth and of evolution. This is life. This is experience. This is being God in action, as you understand it.


## SOUL BALANCING

We wish to bring your attention to the fact that the reason various souls who are in a state of imbalance are not able to remain in any one area or another, one dimension or another, and must transgress into the various planes of action where they are not abiding is because they have not integrated within themselves these various faculties and functions and understandings.

Where you are not integrated sufficiently on the Earth with your conscious application, your subconscious knowledge and your superconscious realities, you are not remained anchored, steadfast and suitably functioning on the Earth. Your soul and your spirit are not in harmony with your body or material function, therefore you are imbalanced and out of the proper place and orbit.

Yes indeed, you may be functioning extremely well on what you call a physical, mortal life, but you are not a balanced individual from the point of view of your own creative faculties and your own spiritual consciousness of your destiny. There is no peace within, regardless of what the outer, seeming structure may be and regardless of how much power you may exercise over other life forms and your fellow human beings.

Carrying this extension of thought and idea into the next plane of action, we wish you to recognize that as many astral forces or beings who have made the transition, or have left their physical

98

bodies, are equally imbalanced and are in a state of turmoil as you find upon the Earth plane. Therefore, they are not satisfied, peaceful and exercising, in the same manner that those on Earth are not who are of the nonintegrated variety. So, where do they exercise their powers, their initiatives and their understandings? Both on the astral and on the Earth. This is where you have made many, many mistakes and have much to learn and require much patience in order to reabsorb and to rework this condition.

If you will not see and will not understand that these individuals, who are Earthbound and influencing Earth, come into your orbit and exercise their imbalanced conditions upon your plane and planet, through you in many cases when you are open and are nonreceptive to spiritual ideas and balancing, integrated understandings, then you have a great deal to learn and to comprehend, because this is a fact.

## INTEGRATION OF EXPERIENCES

All the principles that are within you, all the experiences that you have had opened to your consciousness, are at play at all times. Our function and job are to integrate them so they become whole, balanced and useful functioning for the total entity or unit which you are as an individualization of the God Self.

But this is not operable through all the planes and the planets of this solar system at one time. It is a never-ending process and progress. That is why you have evolution and the various forms of incarnational experience in a long-range period of time. Patience is the prerequisite here, of course; your patience in understanding this, your patience in accepting this, and then your patience in exercising it without becoming impatient, because you come to understand the divine principle and the unity of purpose that are behind all things.

In an example here, let us say you are incarnated on a planet of a very high evolutionary grace and understanding, but your memory recall is opened unto your Earth experiences and even unto the errors you may have created in past lives elsewhere in and through this solar system. The fact that you are in the process of reanalyzing and rebalancing them in order to integrate them into one whole dedication, purpose and function is the very reason you are incarnated on that planet of a high evolvement.

In the process of integrating and learning and unifying all these experiences is life, is the life experience, is the life realization, is the stretching toward and unifying with the original God Source of

99

your Self. There again, the trinity principle is not a separating principle, where you realize you are an individualization or son of the God Force, negative-positive Mother-Father God, but the fact that you recognize you are one in the trinity aspect. All of these things take time and must be done in some place where it is proper to do this.

## LESSONS IN EVERY PLANE

Each one of the places in the planetary structure has its own particular faculty and function and purpose. Just as the Earth planet has a particular lesson that is predominant over all other lessons, so each of the other planes and planets of experience throughout this solar system has its unique purpose, function and plan.

As you go through these various planes and planets you absorb what is their predominant or individualized speciality. By absorbing that speciality you have another ingredient to integrate in your total experience and knowledge and performance. That is why it is so very important for you to understand your lesson, wherever you are, to the very fullest and best of your ability at the time you are there.

Never must you say, when you are on one plane or planet or dimension or another, that you wish you were elsewhere, for this is minimizing the magnetic pull that has put you where you are in the first place and is nullifying to a great degree that which you must learn. For you are not absorbing, you are not integrating and you are not balancing that which already is in you and that which you must incorporate into your total being.

A Christed son, a child of God, must know all there is in the creation of that potential being or individualization. He must come to know and to accept all that is possible within that dimension or area of experience, and all the energy and the function that are possible through his vehicle in which he is expressing at that time on that plane of action. As he then goes into other areas he takes with him a total, complete and harmonious, peaceful, conscious awareness of what is involved, and there is no conflict when he moves on to other areas of expression and needs of expansion.

This must be principally understood at this time, because as you go from the Earth plane consciousness where you are at the present time and develop a harmonious relationship with those astral forces that need lifting, harmonizing and integrating with what has been involved upon the Earth for millions of years and reach toward your etheric or spiritual consciousness of God Self, you are responding to a total balance of the trinity action in yourself where you are now.

The physical or conscious mind or body relates to that aspect of you in which you express a three-dimensional vehicle. The astral experiences relate to all the memory patterns of all dimensions and planes throughout this solar system as you have experienced them in one life's incarnation or another. The etheric or spiritual Sonship consciousness or area of development relates to your powers, talents and abilities to integrate all of these faculties.

## DOMINION OF MAN

So, without one or the other you are imbalanced, you are not whole, you are not fulfilling the function for which you were created. And you certainly are not expressing God in the highest form, because God is integrated, God is one, God is all, and therefore all is in that one Consciousness. Can you comprehend and accept this? For without it you will not proceed in the manner in which it is intended for you to proceed upon this planet in introducing the God consciousness for the next era of evolution which is to come in the Aquarian Age with the return of Sananda, who is Jesus the Christ and Prince of this planet and who demonstrated this integrating consciousness and this faculty and ability to have dominion over all forces, including those forces which you call the Luciferian or devils.

Let us remind you that there was never a time when these negative forces or areas of consciousness which you call the devil intimidated or had any power whatever over that one who is known as the Christ of this planet. At all times he was able to see and to know these error conditions and thoughts and to remove them from not only his own activities, such as in the temptation of the wilderness, but from the consciousness and the activities of all other individuals who were subjected to that power due to their own imbalance.

This was the demonstration and is the demonstration of the Christed, unified Son-of-God consciousness. It must become yours, as well. For there is nothing that has power over you except that you give it power and allow it to have any dominion in your consciousness.

## INTEGRATION WITH LIGHT BODY

It is this Sonship, and this reality of all things being one and equalized and balanced, each having its function and place, and

101

ability to be dissolved if undesirable and unworthy, that comes with Christ consciousness and the light-body function. In order to express the light body upon the Earth plane, you must have integrated and have balanced all of these faculties within yourself. Until you have them totally balanced and integrated you cannot express the light body or the resurrected form of your Sonship and spiritual consciousness on and in and through the Earth projection.

Until you can see this and experience it within your own consciousness, you will not be able deliberately to accept this higher function and thereby dissolve the lower or lesser function. The Earth body is created in order to learn this lesson. It is held in place and in orbital frequency by its own molecular structure because it has the properties within it to keep balanced all of these areas and elements which are involved in your being while on the structure known as the planet Earth.

Then, as the light body is introduced because you have reached up and out into the higher realms and can accept their functioning, talents and purposes, you will dissolve, or will superimpose or will integrate that light body with, that physical structure and the two shall become as one. This is the wedding or the marriage of the superconscious with the conscious and subconscious self.

First of all, your conscious and your subconscious must become wedded sufficiently and integrated sufficiently while in the Earth body so you absorb all the astral entities, experiences, knowledges and memory patterns in your conscious mind, are aware of them and in total balance and harmony within yourself. This is what we refer to as the soul cleansing and the elimination of negative karma and the exercise of positive karma; karma being the effects you are rewarded or contend with due to the causes that you have put into place, that you have put into motion.

When the marriage of the conscious and the subconscious is in total harmony and balance, then the integrating force of your spiritual awareness or your etheric light-body comes and superimposes over that area and the two become one again. Whereas they never were separated, they are able to operate harmoniously in and through that dimension and experience.

So, we have tried to explain to you here that as you see and sense the separation because of your varied and multiple experiences everywhere throughout time and place, particularly we refer here to this solar system, you must bring into balance and harmony first the physical form, then the subconscious memory pattern which is related to your astral being and your astral experiences, and then over that will come the superstructure or the superharmonious elements of your light body or resurrected form as it relates to the etheric consciousness.

## UNITY WITH LIGHT FORCES

You are not in control of all of these activities, but your cooperation is in control of all of them. You are subjected at this time in your evolutionary pattern to seeing and cooperating with those elements or those entities known to you as the angelic forces.

Here again we bring you into a new area of comprehension and understanding and ask you to resolve slowly the balance, the harmony and the integration with that. You must at all times recognize the varied and multiple means of Spirit in action, in creating all kinds and all means of expressing Itself through other areas, kingdoms and creations.

You, as a son of God in the Son-of-God consciousness, which is your God or Christ Self, must know how to implement your own powers and functions with those of the duties and the responsibilities of other forms and forces of creation. You must integrate and unify with all light force. Otherwise, you are not unified with God.

That is the potential and the problem of man in action at this time on the human plane. He is not integrated even with the simple elements of the planet on which he is operating. But as he supersedes these areas of experience and exploration he comes into contact with the higher forces and the more subtle forces, even those that exist on the planet or the plane where he is expressing and having his experience.

So, as we go forward into this new knowledge and accept this new area of consciousness we must come into a unified and harmonious balance, a relationship of unity and grace that exists between all of God's creation. Here I am referring to the forces of the astral with the physical, with the angelic, and with the sons of God who are masters ascended beyond the physical, astral, and into the etheric planes and planets of your solar system.

## MAN IS NOT ALONE

Here you must come to accept and to know that these energies and entities or individualizations exist as fully and as consciously and as completely as you think you are existing through a so-called physical body with a mortal mind; and a consciousness of superiority, because you have come in contact with the God Self within.

Remember always, you are not alone, you are not all-powerful and you are not total in yourself or in your own individualization of that God Self. This error condition has existed even upon this planet for many eons of time, regardless of how highly evolved some have become while in the Earth body and in the Earth consciousness.

Many who suppose to have this God consciousness and mastership over the physical body, over the astral planes, and some sense of their etheric reality, do not comprehend, do not appreciate and do not integrate their force with all the other creative principles and energies that are existing throughout this area of development which we term here as the solar system, for this is all we are involved with at this particular time.

As you grow and expand in other areas of consciousness, you will come to a more universal understanding of many creatures, of many forces in the superior planes beyond those involved in our present solar system, and will work consciously with them for what they can contribute and aid you in. Until this can be done the unification and the oneness and the reality of the God-is-all level of mentality cannot be fully appreciated and exercised.

This is all we require of you, this is all we ask of you: the fact that you do not deny the other forms of creation being as willing and as wonderful as your own. This is all that is required of you at this time. Later, as you gain power and stature over your own self and with your own higher Self, you can come into comparisons and learn from all other life forms and forces, to your own benefit and participation.

## KNOWING ONE'S SELF

That you are not capable of exercising these privileges at this time is obvious; and unfortunate, because you could gain much from them and would gain much in the building up of your own ego consciousness at this time in your development, and be greatly enhanced by the awareness of their specialities and individualities. For remember, as you are concentrating on knowing your Self, so are all other life forms concentrating on knowing themselves.

In this case we refer to the knowing of your Self as knowing those potentials, those peculiarities of function, those individualizations of the one integrating God Force above all things, Which created all things. In another sense of knowing your Self, of course, we refer to knowing the God Energy Force, the unifying single principle of all things; for those are two levels of awareness and two aspects of the same principle.

But know your Self where you are now. Know what your job and your function are where you are now. Know that there is an endless area and potential for experience. So, go ahead with joy and pleasure in learning all that is presented to you at each step of your evolutionary progress.

But know too that until you are integrated with all the other aspects yearning and growing equally, but independently from you, and eventually to be integrated into your knowledge and experience, even if only by observation and communion, then you are not whole and one with the God Force Which created you and all else that does exist.

For in the consciousness or the awareness of God, as you call Him, there is all. All exist equally, all are created equally, all have equal potential for knowing and returning unto their Source, and expressing that individualization or uniqueness of that magnificent and ever-changing but unchanging law of God in action, which is love. Amen.

I am Raphael, integrating these thoughts in your consciousness as much as you will permit, and hoping to give you that responsibility throughout all eternity as you grow into the job and into the function and can accept that responsibility which is now mine and which I must adhere to and protect. All is well. God is good. I am in Him, as you are. Therefore, we are one.

# 10. UNIFICATION FOR NEW CREATION

## ANGELIC INSTRUCTION

Because the majority of your time in the remainder of this period called Mark Age sequence of the program is to implement coordination and cooperation of interrelating forces, we, the archangels of the Fourth and the Fifth Rays, wish to spend our time and energy preparing and instructing you about the fullness of unification and the creation of new form out of that unification.

You will be given enough insight to work with these independent, unified, diverse forces and molecular structures, to see and to appreciate the fact that much is involved in your own application: first, for your own ongoing and spiritual evolution as an individualization of the unit of God, the Self involved in matter, time and place; second, the re-order of your thinking in relationship to others of your own kind in the race of man; third, becoming part of the planet and all of its forces and energies that reconstitute its makeup; and fourth, the interplanetary, interdimensional rest of creative principals who become attached to, work through and relate themselves in time and space to your ongoing and specifications.

Your methods for doing this are first of all in mind and in love. Then, with deliberate applied energy and plan you can become more select in those relationships for yourselves and others, bringing about a new form, a new life style, a new purpose to the planetary structure and evolvement as it befits the sons of God who are governors and controllers of life energy and the forces that express in that place and time where you are residing.

It is not without due consideration and proper preparation that these steps have been given to you. But it is with divine guidance and the understanding that all that is shared is for the benefit of all who give it, who receive it, who share it, and then who pass it on for others to use. It is not ours alone to understand and to work with these principles, but it is ours to demonstrate them and to teach them so you can do the same in your turn and for your own spiritual progress as it is now occurring upon the planet Earth.

## I AM CONSCIOUSNESS

I Am, the spokesman for all parts of yourself in whatever re-joining circumstances occur beneath the soul. The spirit Self, this is the fundamental control—device, if you want to call it that—that we concern ourselves with here. The I Am Self, over and above all subsequent series of expressions, gives the key and gives the code and the pace by which these unfolding steps may occur. Because you are to adhere only to the I Am principle within yourself and your own individualization of the I Am presence, then you may proceed in these normal instructions and developments as we here give them.

First and foremost we become aware of the fact that other energies are existing and must be balanced within our own consciousness and acceptance of them. As we reach out and seek these other individualizations or forms of creation, we recognize through the intellectual reasoning and the subconscious memory patterns of the soul what they are, what place they play, what form and function they must take in our interrelating processes.

This balancing of conditions and modular matters is ever present in the I Am consciousness, is ever present in the soul recording device of the spiritual man. He then knows what to avoid, what to seek and with what to coordinate. This becomes necessary as he understands his evolving and his ongoing problems, as it entails deeper analysis and greater functions and expanded opportunities.

Within this balancing of the Fifth Ray concept, as already outlined previously, he who is aware of these developments and entity expressions works toward them by magnetic attraction, or avoids them by screening out or protecting himself from that which will not be applicable to the present problem or the present function that is involved in his development. This is as far as the individualization of each is concerned.

## RACE INVOLVEMENT

But when it comes to the race structure or the species involved, more must be analyzed, more must be realized and much more must be accepted, so that if it is for the good of the whole to experience and to withdraw from that episode or interrelationship, then that is the proper procedure. However, on the other hand, if a sacrifice must be made, then many individualized Christ consciousnesses must devote themselves to that.

But when more are involved and experience the mastership of these things, then the choice can be made more selectively and more perfectly than it has been up until this time in this present solar system. Particularly on this present planet, since the fall of man indicated that his choice was an error one and inbuilt in his subconscious track as a race or what you call group subconsciousness, are the fact and the memory of the error and of the deep scar caused by that episode.

You still are not completely out of the depth of that despair, and will not be for the rest of this century, as you term it, because you are in the process of working these things out in soul memory, in race consciousness, and paying off the debts of all which has been incurred and not balanced properly.

Can you not see and not understand and not accept the fact that all this upheaval and turmoil you are experiencing as a race, in the planetary sense, is caused by this original sin of falling away from truth and not knowing the light and not working in the spiritual manner in which you were intended and for which you have forfeited so much during these ensuing eras and civilizations of time?

## ALIGNMENT WITH ANGELS

But balance must be. Balance must be kept. Integration of the various forces is the result. In this interlevel, interplanetary, interdimensional exchange of thought, of experience and of memory within the entire race of man now as he is evolving, we have the opportunity to bring about new thought forms, new desires from those thought forms, and consequently the new being or planetary structure or form, which is the responsibility of man with the aid of his angelic co-participants or partners. Then we must become aligned in our co-function, for this is fundamentally the purpose and the project of this entire series of informational discourses to you now.

It cannot be any longer that you disregard the existence of planetary forces, angelic, devic, elemental kingdoms, and the total responsibility of the race of man as a Son of God, which he is; the Christ in action upon Earth and in the solar system and eventually beyond that.

That the interrelating, corresponding thoughts, desires and deeds which then occur from out of this will bring about that new form— or, as the scriptures say, a new heaven upon a new Earth—is the basic and fundamental urging that we are required to prod and to bring about in the time sequence known as the Aquarian Age.

That we will have every assistance in this is also part of the plan, and the Hierarchy's responsibility as it concerns this planet and this entire solar system. For as you have been taught and have been led to conceive of in this instruction book, there are many planes, planets, dimensions involved in the ongoing race of man as he expresses now in the third dimensional form known as Earth.

But because he will balance all this error, will pay off all his karmic debt, will reconstitute his thinking to include his soul experiences with his physical consciousness and body, along with the overriding and constant principle of the I Am Self who is the spirit or Christ individualization within himself, we can proceed in a more normal, progressive unfolding of this information and then the ensuing results of that.

## READY FOR NEW EARTH

But first we begin with you yourselves. Then we involve you with the others of like mind, since you will be attracted magnetically to those who have received the same information, have worked on the same concepts, have developed the same deeds, and have the same goals in mind for the new heaven upon a new Earth.

The new Earth will be your new bodies and the new heaven will be that balance and total concept of all that is involved in the heavenly spheres—or the spiritual spheres, if you prefer—that include the angelic forces as well as the higher race, or the Elder brothers, who came with the angelic realm to prepare this planet in the first place.

That refers to many eons past and is not the problem that is before you at this very moment. But it constitutes the background in history of this planet and its destructive tendencies in the recent civilizations and contracts. You may not go for ever and ever in a wrong direction without coming to the conclusion that you are getting absolutely nowhere, which is what the race of man has come to at this point. Many of you may think and feel in your own individual reasoning minds that man has not reached this conclusion, or a sufficient number of men on the planet at this time have not reached this conclusion: that they have reached a dead end.

But believe us, and seek this knowledge for yourselves, the majority which reside on the Earth know, feel and are resolved to turn about-face from where they have been heading as individualized souls and as an entire race. That you will begin to effect an influence upon this thinking and will proceed to form the right patterns in thought, in word and in deed is the obligation of the hundred and forty-four thousand light workers who will demonstrate the new body in and through the third dimensional planet as it expresses now.

## 144,000 LIGHT DEMONSTRATORS

It is this coming together or fusing—let us say, the integrating principle of the Fifth Ray step of which I, Raphael, am in charge—that shall cause enough energy, through thought matter, to bring about Gabriel's fourth step of materialization and crystallization of the new form and body. This again involves the new body or the new form of light through the spiritual structure for each individualized self or cell in that race of man, as well as to provide a pattern by which all the race may pass through.

By integrating thus with the angelic forces, those of the hundred and forty-four thousand who are the light workers in the advance guard of this program and plan can show and will develop that co-partnership and co-participation of which we spoke, of two levels of God's kingdoms and creations to reconstitute the planet, and to prepare the entire solar system for its ongoing into evolutionary procedures as well. It cannot be otherwise. The new Earth is connected with the new heaven. In this term in this way you can conceive the heaven as including all the other planets, planes and dimensions of this particular solar system.

Since this will be affected by what you do on Earth, then it follows, as you can see clearly, the new heaven of that immediate vicinity you call your solar system. But how much more will it involve also the heavens beyond those heavens; and galaxies, universes on endlessly into infinity. We try to bring you this in a small measure only to help and to encourage you that each drop of water in the ocean affects the entire ocean, and that the ocean itself, in its processes and purposes and beingness, contributes to every drop of water that is within it.

This interrelating, integrating, cohesive force cannot be emphasized enough, cannot be contemplated frequently enough by you in order for it to manifest and to bring about the desired result, which is a new form, a new body, a new concept, a new entity for the creation known as mankind, who is the Son of God, the Christ in form.

It is again that we emphasize this form, for we are concerned

**110**

with the light-body structure, or the superimposing of the I Am Self vehicle over all that exists upon the Earth at this time. In the end days these demonstrations and executions of the spiritual body or resurrected form will be the predominant concern and most attractive aspect of your purpose and program in unfolding the rest of mankind—or, let us say, in awakening the rest of mankind—to his own purpose and destiny.

For you truly have laggards among you. There are many who have come to learn these lessons and to be awakened while upon the Earth. But you may not conquer all their minds and hearts at one time. It will be a gradual process. In the meantime, those souls who are being introduced into the Earth at this time from other planes and planets in the solar system are those who will aid you greatly in this process.

So, the job is not one of your own doing or one of your own exemplifying and energizing, but is one with which you cooperate to the fullest extent and to the greatest amount of your own conception of what is involved here as it is outlined, as it has been given in instruction, as it has been taught and has been given out through the various prophets, channels and mediums of this age we call the Mark Age or the latter-day period.

It is not without preparation. It is not a sudden and unexperimental program, but one with great deliberation and one with great practice; even, may we add, with great failure in the past eras and civilizations of time known upon the planet, particularly those of Lemuria and Atlantis, which have been hidden in the annals of your recorded time, but not hidden to the memory patterns of your soul progress as a race incarnated upon the Earth at this time.

## MEMORY RECALL

In the end days all things will be uncovered and will be rediscovered so you can work with them, reanalyze them, and reconstitute them by rebalancing them. Again we show you how the rebalancing of the Fifth Ray step and my participation as Raphael must be considered and worked with cooperatively, because you on Earth, all of these memory patterns and these definite clues and anthropological and archeological exact facts will have the thought ranges of good and bad, positive and negative, in every degree of them, come forth into race consciousness and memory for each individual involved, and for the race, to accept or to reject.

111

Yes indeed, you will have many recalling their past lives when the evidence is presented to them even in a physical way. Some are having recall of past lives and experiences merely by the presence of these discourses and channelings. Through our efforts you then are being given the opportunity of recalling many of the experiences and the experiments of mankind as he evolved with the planet, for the planet, and helped to develop its various kingdoms by his own thought control.

Let us tell you one simple experiment that is being performed upon the race of man in his memory recall at this time. You have among you some who preach and teach that man has been evolved out of the mineral, the vegetable and the animal kingdoms and eventually became what he is today, to go on to further evolutions. This is totally erroneous, as we already have channeled and have developed in previous books and discourses.

However, what is not recognized by many of these teachers is the fact that in the spiritual consciousness and in the lower astral form, man is capable of introducing himself for a short period of time to any one of those kingdoms and participating in those kingdoms. The lower or the lesser he is in the planes of consciousness at the time, the easier and the quicker it is for him to experience in those lesser and lower kingdoms.

In other words, if one is incorporated into a suspended state upon the astral planes between incarnations and growth development, he easily can imbed himself in a rock, in a tree or in a bird, if we want to give just these types of specific examples.

Thus, in the memory recall as he is evolving back up through those experiences, as his astral body and consciousness are opened up further and further to pass through those experiences, to expose him to those experiences and to lift him back up into his I Am consciousness, he does recall that experience or experiment which he permitted himself in the long evolutionary period and process of learning his natural talents and inherent growth and graces as a son of God during the many eons past when this was permitted. And if he had any reasonable or deliberate problems to work out with this experience, the impaction of it is so great upon the soul record that he would bring forth in his memory consciously the fact that this was a period of existence.

So, it is possible for an individual, in great sincerity and in spiritual yearning and growth, to see himself in some past incarnation as a bird or a tree or part of the mineral pattern of Earth. But this is not a part of his evolution. It is part of a fragmented experience in time and place when he was waiting for further spiritual, divine guidance and evolvement.

112

Many such experiences have occurred throughout all the planes and the planets of this solar system for all of you who are part of the race of man. For man is thirsty for knowledge. Man is obliged to experience life in all of its form. Man must learn to integrate with all the various levels of consciousness and with all the various forms of life that do touch upon and participate in his ongoing and in his evolutionary experience through the varied dimensions, planes and planets of what we call this solar system.

Therefore, to have the memory recall of it and to have fragmented visions, dreams and inner plane concepts about them is really a positive process and not a negative process, if you can look at it in the proper perspective of what it has been and what meaning and bearing it has upon your total experience and your total realization as an integrating force with all other forces and molecular structures as they are designed by you and by us as your co-partners and co-participators in this process of developing form, and place in which form can experience.

Let us look also at another aspect of this. Many times an individualization of the spiritual Self, along with several who are conceiving of the same idea and pattern, will congregate, will integrate, will unify and will experiment to create a form or a place of residence, to have a form and to go on in a separated existence from the majority of their fellowmen or fellow beings of that realm and kingdom known as man, the Son of God.

They may spend millions of years, as you would record time, doing this, experimenting with it and trying to make it happen. Yet, all of that energy and time, all of that endeavor will fail because the proper ingredients, the proper balances needed are not forthcoming. In other words, we still must see that in Spirit's divine plan and workings-out, every thought, every desire are not made manifest by the angelic realm under the Fourth Ray aspect of Archangel Gabriel, who must cohesively manifest crystallized thought patterns in a proper relationship of balance with the Fifth Ray.

That is why we have come together at this time to show you the pattern that must be worked out. The Fourth and the Fifth Rays, in this respect, are co-partners and work to bring about form for these ideas and desires created in the minds of man. If it will not have the proper balance and integrating forces, such as you would in a proper chemical formula, you cannot have a creation manifested properly so that it will stay cohesively together and work in any integrating, practical manner for a spiritual lesson and a pragmatic result.

113

If you only will understand this and will appreciate it and will work with it, then you will save yourselves much grief, much time and much in the way of spiritual energy gone amiss. Naturally, nothing is lost; but nothing is gained, either.

## COORDINATION OF ALL

So you see, my beloved children of the light, in giving you this discourse and opening up your consciousnesses to further opportunities and developments of your spiritual talents and goals, we see and we know that every desire you manifest in yourselves, no matter how many co-partners you may find in that, you still must interrelate it, integrate it and work with it with those angelic forces who supersede your decisions until you can be purified enough, objective enough and spiritualized enough in the cosmic sense to bring about and to desire only those things of the highest good for all of mankind.

In other words, we are not looking for separations and segregated societies of specialized needs. But we are looking for the cohesiveness that will bring all men of the planet Earth, and in this solar system and the dimensions and the planes involved in this solar system, together in one integrating and cohesive force for manifesting the light and for bringing about a coordinated plane and planet that will rest comfortably and peacefully within the entire solar system. That will be the final discourse, by Lord Uriel, to follow. God bless you and keep you. In His name we speak. Amen.

# 11. COORDINATED SERVICE

## UNITY FOR MAJOR PURPOSE

All Seventh Ray workers throughout this solar system must be unified and coordinated for the final rending of the seventh veil and the initiation that shall bring the Earth as a planet into its proper role and function in the solar system of which it is a part and a special, significant aspect or center of love radiation.

This is Archangel Uriel of the Seventh Ray, speaking for Sananda, Nada and all who come under this combination of forces. We speak now not of a single individual, a single aspect of the God consciousness which is the Seventh Ray function, or of single efforts and events, but we speak now of all who participate for the good of the whole and the good of the one purpose.

It is this way in eternal consciousness and spiritual efforts. Never can we assume, when we are in the total comprehension of this grand master plan of Spirit in action, that any one single factor ever is favored or preferred, for that is definitely not the manner in which Spirit works. But Spirit does work in segments, in time periods, and in concentrations of particular formulas, forces, events, jobs to be accomplished; not that any one can consider that every attention and every focus is upon any single event, for this would be ridiculous to conceive.

But when there is an individual purpose or function or event that must be superseding all others in order for it to come into its proper sequence and order and harmony, we can understand that every effort is made toward that goal and special command. It is that of which we speak and alert you.

## SELF-SACRIFICE

Not many are able to put themselves in the position where they devote and donate every ounce of their spiritual affairs to a single individual or purpose which is not of their own evolvement and development. Only when self-sacrifice is entered into the picture

115

of spiritually unfolded consciousnesses can we see the full magnificence and the full manifestation of the Christ Son in action.

So, you have been given this example time and time again, but particularly in that life incarnation when Jesus symbolized his last and final act on Earth as the crucifixion or the sacrificial lamb for the good of all mankind. For if he did not allow himself to be put to the cross at that point, he never could have demonstrated the resurrection of the fleshly form and the ascension which follows.

Nor, if he had not taken all those steps, could he redescend in that fully manifested light body, incorporating the physical structure, as we already have indicated is to take place in the short sequence of events that follow upon this planet Earth, and which we call forth in your imaginations and consciousnesses and endeavors as the final initiation of the Earth planet before stepping into its full Christ role and love radiation for this solar system.

Each is intertwined and intermingled and exploratory for one another, interplaying and formalizing this interchange of energies and awarenesses. As above, so below. As in the macrocosm, so in the microcosm. As Jesus performed for the race of man, so the race of man performs for the planet, so the planet performs for the solar system, and the solar system enacts its proper role and function in the galaxy and the universe of which it is but a single part or cell in the total scheme of all creation.

So, we of the archangel realms serve all who are in the solar system and in creation, as you know it and can even begin to comprehend it. Have we not instilled in your minds now that we serve and work with the lowest form of element or elementals, through the devic kingdoms and the process which creates the form? The form or vehicle we serve to manifest and to bring into balance is the lowest aspect and the least important aspect of your entire beingness as a child of God and a creation of the Divine Source of life, light and love.

But would you understand it if we did not come to you and bring all of this to your attention? And would you serve as we have asked you to serve if we did not indicate that we see there is no job too small, too minute, too detailed to perform for the good of the whole? It is ours to seek the highest and to descend unto the lowest in bringing this about. For none are masters and none are slaves, but all serve the one Source, God almighty, Who is all in all.

## ANGELIC GUIDANCE

That you may begin to comprehend and to work with this is our total endeavor and our only purpose in coming to you in and through this instrument; as we do through many instruments, channels, prophets, and personalized experience in your own dreams, meditations and visions. This must be the way we work, as we cannot work in a physical form on the planet Earth. Therefore, we come to you in and through the forms that already are created and through the various levels of your consciousness that can accept and can work with us and cooperate with us.

We all have indicated to you that now it is absolutely necessary to bring about a proper balance and frequency of consciousness, love, desire, obedience to the frequencies of thought, and the desires that come as a result of those thoughts and new ideas and images which are yours to protect and to project out into the ethers.

By coming together with these various subjects we then can cooperate with you and issue forth the instructions and the power and the desire for those new forms to become made manifest in the areas where they best will serve your highest good and evolutionary experience. But if we did not cooperate with you and did not understand what is necessary, from the cosmic viewpoint, then you could not proceed in the manner in which we have described it here in this book and series of informational discourses.

But since you have been prepared and have been given all that is required for you to know and to understand at this particular point in your conscious awareness, we expect the work to proceed immediately and to unfold in your cosmic consciousness while in Earth embodiment, but going into full Christ frequency; which is the fourth dimensional body or light, resurrected form.

## LIGHT-BODY PATTERN

That form already has been created, as we have indicated to you, through the chohan of the Seventh Ray, known on the Hierarchal Board as Sananda but previously known to Earth consciousness and history as the light of God, Jesus of Nazareth, who came to demonstrate the Christ faculties and functions as regards this planet in a third dimensional frequency form.

Since the pattern has been set and is applicable unto all on the Earth, then each one who can accept this responsibility, can work unselfishly and can make the sacrifices that are necessary for it, will be able to step into a similar form or mold and re-create a similar job, pattern, function and service. But what is more required at this time is that many more together will see it and will do it and will join in the one endeavor, which is to re-create this planet and

117

all life form upon it into its more true and more perfect and more spiritualized senses and subjects.

So, we ask this in the name of those who have come from Seventh Ray demonstrations to begin the activity of solidification, because of their particular affinity to that one who made the sacrifice originally, through many incarnations which are given heretofore. Due to that affinity they can come into a melding by this and can re-create a similar situation, a similar vibratory energy in thought, first of all; then in desire, second of all; then in full manifestation, finally and foremost.

## NEW MANIFESTATION THROUGH LOVE

Let us review how this may be done in the ray of love divine and peace or rest in the cosmic consciousness. You set in motion that mental aspect and image of what is totally desirable and completed through the initiations that preceded the seventh initiation that must come to pass. It has not been completed fully yet. We are in the process of rending the seventh veil and bringing the Earth into its final or seventh initiation.

Resting in this knowledge surely and securely, projecting it out with the peace of mind that comes to all those who know truth and can see no other way but that truth be made manifest in its fullest glory, and with love for the Divine Which created this aspect and fullness and took care of all the previous steps, you properly begin the imaging, the projecting and the satisfaction that must be picked up in the etheric vibration of the consciousness of all men upon the Earth.

The Seventh Ray workers who are on the planet, and all Seventh Ray forces from the archangel myself, Uriel, down through all those who come under my sphere, plus the workers under the chohan or director of Seventh Ray activities on the etheric and the astral vibratory rates, who is known as Sananda or Jesus the Christ, keep this chemicalization or molecular structure of thought ever steadfast and unmoving.

By the desire we manifest or project into that thought pattern and that solidified single image, an energy is activated similarly by causing the motion or the movement of that image to reach into all realms of man's consciousness, whether it be on the Earth or in the astral or on the etheric, and all dimensions that concern this solar system as they relate to the Earth planet.

The love that activates from this thought and desire is what brings it into actual full manifestation. By bringing these three aspects together, or the trinity of spiritual consciousness—which is one consciousness, of course—we complete the rending of the seven phases of the seventh veil and allow the seventh initiation, which is the full Christ consciousness for all men upon the Earth, to become manifested in its proper time sequence and the events that will be orderly and for the highest good of each one who is involved and who will experience that.

## LAW OF SACRIFICE

But you well may ask about all those workers who operate under the other faculties and functions and knowledge of the first six rays: (1) will and power; (2) intelligence and wisdom; (3) personal love, feeling and desire of service; (4) the crystallization and the manifestation of life form and expression in a third, going into fourth, dimensional frequency; (5) the integration and the unity of whole balance for all of these aspects; and (6) the most important for the age you are in now, the latter-day period, this which is transmutation, purification, and the change that can manifest for a Seventh Ray or a final step.

The Seventh Ray workers provide the mold or the area by which all of these can come into solidified unification and oneness, operating each in his own unique and particular way for the good of the whole. As stated here quickly, to know and to realize the sacrifice each makes to bring into manifestation the benefit of the one which is to be comprehended and clearly defined are the fullness and the fulfillment of the seventh step for each one of those workers who come under the other influences and project their own unique and individual services.

In other words, they cannot fulfill their own functions and exercise their own highest aspects unless they learn to use the sacrificial element within themselves for the good of one outside of themselves. This is truth. This is how truth is served. This is the law and the manifestation of that law in any plane of spiritual action. When you do not have this quality in operation, and ones who are endeavoring to express spiritual life and comprehension do not see fit to adhere and to cooperate with one another, as outlined and described, they cause a much-explicit division of will and purpose in manifestation.

In the first place, the will is the divine will that must be served, as it is exemplified by the First Ray in El Morya, and in Lord Michael as the archangel and the titular head of this entire solar system for this one event. If the will of God is not served in each and every one first and foremost and primarily above any other consideration, then he truly is not expressing divinity in himself or in his aspect or with those for whom he is responsible, either as an archangel or as a chohan or as a spiritual missionary, wherever he may be expressing.

## ANGELIC SACRIFICES

In the instance, for an example, of Lord Michael and myself as Uriel, you have a typical example of ones who are willing and able to sacrifice the many and multiple roles, functions and missions throughout the great conglomerate of eternal creation and expression for the good of a small, tiny segment of mankind, and even a smaller segment of God's total creation.

Let us look for a single instant at the vastness of our roles and missions in protecting and working with the elements of all dimensions in this universe in order to create form, and to keep them in a juxtaposition of total balance and harmony in order for all creative form to take place and to interrelate and to have integrating opportunities, expanding out, withdrawing, relating, functioning, dissolving and transmuting into other, higher aspects.

Since we are concerned—and when I say *we* here, I mean all the forces that come under our direction—with these multiple roles, missions, functions and consciousnesses within the solar system, the galaxy and this entire universe in which they are a part, we still can sacrifice a great deal of our ongoing and our responsibility and our concentration of forces, regarding that one small segment of this individual planet, because it needs and requires our total concentration and effort for this particular time period or sequence of events known as the latter-day period, and the Golden Era to come of the Age of Aquarius.

A two-thousand-year program and a three-thousand-year program have been unfolded unto your awareness. Not in great detail, it is true, but enough to give you the stimulation of thought and a willingness to make sure that they can manifest in their most perfect and most harmonious way. Still, two thousand or three thousand years in eternity is as nothing but the winking of the eye of God, as they say. So, we see it as such. And we have not withdrawn our efforts and our attention, our thoughts and our powers from everywhere else in cosmic time and place for this one sequence of events.

But since we know the urgency and the emergency that are involved in the latter-day period—or the Mark Age period and program, as we like to call it—here upon this planet Earth, and the small segment of the fallen race of man which must evolve back up into his rightful place and heritage as a son of God and create his own new form with our aid and assistance, then we willingly give every ounce of energy, every concentration of thought, every ability and instruction within our power to do.

It is thus that Lord Michael, who is surely concerned with much more in and through this universe, particularly as it relates to the ongoing of the race of man and the Elder race who are not subjected to the same trials, tribulations, cleansings, responsibilities and karmic debts that you who are on the Earth are concerned with, can and does come for a long, protracted period of time to serve as the titular head of this solar system's governing body called the Hierarchal Board, so that many in the race of man and those who have prepared themselves as the Elder race in their light-body-frequency function can take over that segment of responsibility, can learn those functions and jobs, and release him and his forces to those of other areas in the creative aspects of the will of God, the truth and the law and the sword which must be applied to keep all things in balance and in unity and harmony for the divine Father-Mother God Who expresses through the Son-love rays.

## MUST EXPRESS GOD SEED

Your knowledge is minuscule. Your powers are unopened. Your functions are limited. And yet, the tantalizing responsibilities are put before you in order to awaken what within is inherent and possible. Because you are a child, a son, a full co-creator with that Divine Energy that made you and prepared you and seeks you out at this moment, you may never rest in the place where you are now.

For this broadcast stimulates, awakens and reminds you constantly that what is within must express without. That means, particularly and precisely, that that which is within you as a seed, your own God consciousness, must express outwardly. Whether or not you wish to accept this or to work with it or to cooperate with those who will bring it about is not really up to you individually, but is placed totally before the race of man to whom this broadcast is being made now.

As this channel is connected to the Seventh Ray function, and works in harmony and partnership totally in and through the force field of El Morya, who is incarnated with her in physical embodiment to bring this about, the two act as a combined force field of energy that never can resist the higher plane call and formula that speak first of all through the First Ray of Will and divine idea in manifested fullness through the Seventh Ray aspect of acceptance; the receptacle, let us say, of femininity in action, or the mother aspect of the Seventh Ray which rests peaceful in knowledge and content at the completion of all that has gone before, and in divine love combined with divine will never can submerge or still that formulated matter which we call the hierarchal plan and program as benefit and befit the Earth planet.

For this is not a role or a mission of individuals. This is not a function of self-will. This is not anything that can be conjured or controlled by conscious mind or personality incarnational aspects. Since it has to be a combined, cooperative venture of spiritualized forces, energies and emulations, it comes to pass as long as the conscious mind holds forth the willingness to become that which is the fullness of the creative principle that lies within, or the seed of God which is planted herein, and by acceptance of it. Unless you likewise are able to emulate a similar function for your own individualized will, broadcast, energy and area of service, you cannot be brought into the cojoining of this operation and function as concerns the Earth planet.

## SERVE ALL FOR RACE EVOLUTION

Let us be very clear in understanding what is involved. If any think that the Earth planet, though it be the least and the smallest member of the society of planets in this solar system, can be eliminated or disregarded or overridden in the ongoing spiritual evolution of the race of man in the solar system, he is seriously mistaken about it.

For, as already indicated and brought out in this broadcast, and last and final instruction regarding this phase of your work, you are to serve the least in order to receive the highest adulation and acceptance and fulfillment of that which you strive for as the race of man and the Son of God, which is the Christ consciousness and body of love from the Father-Mother God Which created it originally.

In other words, and most specifically and without equivocation or dissection, you cannot come into your full role and mission anywhere without being part of this activity. Where you are and how you do it are certainly up to your conscious will and attention at this time.

So, this broadcast goes out. So, this instruction goes out. So, this declaration of faith and understanding and will, with divine love in operation, must be made manifest everywhere throughout this Earth or the astral planes involved with the Earth, the dimensions that connect throughout the solar system, and the planets and the planes of operation of spiritual consciousness, etherically, astrally and celestially speaking.

We speak unto those who are of the Luciferian forces as well, for they helped to create this dimension, this plane and this planet of activity for the disregarding of this one edict that came out of the Godhead originally and purposely before this time of *now* and this long history of Earth and man upon it. They too know and understand and receive all which has gone forth.

So, as long as we have the two in one—Seventh Ray function in total cooperation and coordination with First Ray function, divine will and the sword of truth—we cannot escape the ensuing results that must come to pass upon the Earth and throughout the solar system and all environs connected with it in the next thirty-to-forty-year period of time; because, as we already have indicated, this thirty-to-forty-year period of time affects all the history of mankind in this solar system for the next three-thousand-year period of time, because without the smallest and most minute link in the chain, the chain cannot become strengthened and grow where it is intended to grow and to expand and to serve in the long chain of events and circumstances and time sequences of life force.

Let us not misunderstand, let us not work against the grain of, these things. Let us solidify our intentions. Let us come into the unification of principle and truth which prevails within us. For within each one, regardless of his station, his evolvement or his form of creation, right from the angelic realms through to the very basic elements that are involved in creating a form through which each one may operate and express, we know the truth, we have seen the truth, we are feeling the truth, and therefore we must express the love of truth in order for the form to be made manifest.

## SEPARATION TIME

Until all can recognize that this is truth and willingly cooperate with it, from the highest to the lowest energy expression in himself and herself as of now, we will not gain all those souls and have all in a cooperative, unified whole. But we understand and we accept the failures that may still entail, and hold out for their own free-will expression.

We can accept those who will not accept us and these cries of joy and fulfillment that lie ahead. But we cannot correlate and absorb their energy in the process with which we are involved in a concentrated series of efforts at this time. We will have to be very select, as already indicated previously in these discourses, as to how we go about the fulfillment of what comes next.

This is not up to you to discern and to select from your own conscious evolvement, for that would be a serious error and fault at this particular stage of the game of unfoldment. What we must do is to know and to accept the fact that many will not be able to adhere to these principles and shall have to be released to other places and climes of expression. These are being provided for at the present time. So shall you see many who do not join you in the endeavors of what we have described and have outlined here.

By this we do not mean you will see it in the present consciousness, or even in the present incarnation of time and in what we call the Mark Age period and program upon the Earth, as regards the next thirty or forty years of unfolding developments and events. But we do mean to prepare your minds, your souls for the spiritual evolutionary comparisons that shall leave some in the focus and the picture of a New Age with a new heaven and a new Earth, as we described it, and some out of focus or out of the range of this development and experience as you will accept and will work with it in the times to come ahead, what we call the next three-thousand-year period or program.

Be not alarmed by these things. For, as we have said, there is no final damnation or extermination of an individualized part of God, or of any soul who has sought to express himself and to become part of that spiritual energy. None are lost. But each species will be judged. And each individual soul must be judged by his own Christ Self from within. This is part of the responsibility of the guardian angels and of the individualized I Am Self within each person, as you regard individuals.

But since this is not the immediate period for that function and is not the immediate concern for those who are residing upon the Earth planet at this time, since they have much more to do and to be concerned with at the present regarding their own salvation and the salvation of the Earth planet in these latter-day periods, we ask you not to dwell too long upon these thoughts and these proclamations.

The fact remains, however, that it is our responsibility to instruct you of what part is played by those who will not accept, as well as to instruct you about the part you will play in, the ensuing and unfolding events as they must occur here and now, since this program is now in effect immediately and as of this proclamation.

## URIEL WITH ALL

I am Uriel, assigned unto this planet Earth until the final fruition of its Seventh Ray initiation herein described. The love radiation of planet Earth must be so unified with that of Seventh Ray functions through and with all Seventh Ray workers that I, in my function and role as the archangel of all who come under that aspect, adhere to the principles of divine law and will and express myself in all who are upon the planet, regardless of what ray, what function, what level of consciousness they appear to express at the present moment.

It must be so that I sacrifice myself, my forces, my energies, my understandings to this need. Unless it is done from the fullest compassion and completion of all that has gone before, we cannot bring the last into the first; Which is God, the one and only, the single, the whole, the Almighty, the purpose for our total existence. Amen. God be with you, as He is in you and in me, Uriel. All is one, one, one: one God, one Life Force, one truth expressed in the one race or son of man.

# THE SEVEN DIVINE ATTRIBUTES OR ELOHIM OR RAYS OF LIFE

| ELOHIM OR IDEA | RAY OR COLOR | DIVINE ATTRIBUTE OR PRINCIPLE | ARCHANGEL IN CHARGE | CHOHAN OR DIRECTOR | MAN'S EARTHLY APPLICATION |
|---|---|---|---|---|---|
| First | Blue | Law or will; the word of God. | Michael | El Morya | Speaking the word for Spirit. Using sword (words) of truth for spiritual purposes. |
| Second | Yellow | Mind, intelligence, thoughts of God. | Jophiel (Hophiel) | Kut Humi | Intellectual understanding of divine laws, and wisdom in applying them. |
| Third | Pink | Feeling or love nature in God. | Chamuel (replaced Lucifer) | Lanto | Self-dedication and sacrifice to a cause, individual, country, religion. |
| Fourth | Crystal (colorless) | Development or manifested forms of God. | Gabriel | Serapis Bey | Completion or anchoring on physical of ideas and inspirations. |
| Fifth | Green | Integrating, unifying cohesiveness of God. | Raphael | Hilarion | Healing and synthesizing varied modes of expression. Unity in diversity. |
| Sixth | Violet | Transmutability or change of form through God. | Zadkiel | St. Germain | Cleansing, purification, bridging old with new through transformation. |
| Seventh | White & Gold | Rest, peace, God's love for His work, love of His manifestations for Him. Love in action. | Uriel | Sananda | Completion of spiritual lessons on physical plane. Living in divine love, peace, rest. |

# GLOSSARY OF NAMES
# AND NEW AGE TERMS

*Adamic race:* those of the Elder race who descended onto Earth in combination of third and fourth dimensional bodies in attempt to raise their fallen brothers of the human subrace who had become entrapped in the third dimension.

*akashic record:* soul history of an individual, a race, a heavenly body.

*angel:* a being of celestial realms.

*Aquarian Age:* period of approximately two thousand years following the Piscean Age. Cycle during which the solar system moves through the area of cosmic space known as Aquarius.

*archangel:* head of a ray of life in this solar system. First: Michael. Second: Jophiel. Third: Chamuel (replaced Lucifer). Fourth: Gabriel. Fifth: Raphael. Sixth: Zadkiel. Seventh: Uriel.

*Armageddon:* the latter-day, cleansing, harvest, Mark Age period immediately prior to the second coming of Sananda as Christ Jesus. The era wherein man must eliminate the negativity in himself and the world.

*ascended master:* one who has reached the Christ level and who has translated his physical body into the light or etheric body.

*ascension:* spiritual initiation and achievement wherein one translates the physical body into a higher dimension.

*astral:* pertaining to realms or planes between physical and etheric. Lower astral realms approximate Earth plane level of consciousness; higher astral realms approach etheric or Christ realms.

*astral body:* one of the seven bodies of man pertaining to Earth plane life. Appearance is similar to physical body. Upon transition called death it becomes the operative body for the consciousness, in the astral realms.

127

*Atlantis:* civilization springing from Lemuria, dating from 206,000 to 10,000 years ago. Land area was from present eastern part of U.S.A. and the Caribbean to western part of Europe, but not all one land mass. Sinking of Atlantis was from 26,000 to 10,000 years ago; allegory of Noah and the flood.

*aura:* the force field around an object, especially a person. Contains information graphically revealed in color to those able to see with spiritual vision.

*cause and effect, law of:* as you sow, so shall you reap.

*celestial:* angelic.

*chakra:* a center of energy focus, generally located around one of the seven major endocrine glands, but which penetrates the other, more subtle, bodies.

*Chamuel:* Archangel at head of the Third Ray, replacing Lucifer.

*channel:* a person who is used to transmit communications, energies, thoughts, deeds by either Spirit or an agent of Spirit. Also called prophet, sensitive, recorder, medium, instrument.

*chohans:* directors of the seven rays of life, under the archangels. First: El Morya. Second: Kut Humi. Third: Lanto. Fourth: Serapis Bey. Fifth: Hilarion. Sixth: St. Germain. Seventh: Sananda with Nada. As channeled through Yolanda numerous times.

*Christ:* a title indicating achievement of the spiritual consciousness of a son of God. Also refers to the entire race of man as and when operating in that level of consciousness.

*Christ awareness:* awareness of the Christ level within one's self and of the potential to achieve such.

*Christ consciousness:* achievement of some degree of understanding and use of spiritual powers and talents.

*Christ Self:* the superconscious, I Am, higher Self, oversoul level of consciousness.

*conscious mind:* the mortal level of one's total consciousness; which is about one tenth of such total consciousness. Usually refers to the rational, thinking aspect in man.

*consciousness, mass:* collective consciousness of race of man on Earth, all planes or realms pertaining to Earth.

*coordination unit:* designation and function of Mark-Age unit, Coordination Unit #7 for the Hierarchal Board, pertaining to coordination of light workers and light groups on the Earth plane for the hierarchal plan and program.

*Creative Energy:* a designation for God or Spirit or Creative Force.

128

*death:* transition from physical life or expression on Earth to another realm, such as physical incarnation on some other planet or expression on astral or etheric realms.

*devas:* those intelligent entities of the etheric planes who control the patterns for manifested form in the etheric, Earth and astral planes, under the direction of the angelic kingdom.

*dimension:* a plane or realm of manifestation. A range of frequency vibration expression, such as third dimensional physical on Earth.

*Divine Mind:* God or Spirit; in reality the only mind that exists, man having a consciousness within this one mind.


*Earth:* this planet. When referring to the planet, Mark-Age uses a capital *E,* since it is the only name for this planet that we have been given through interdimensional communications via Yolanda.

*Elder race:* those sons of God who did not become entrapped in the third dimension as the human subrace.

*elect:* one who has been chosen by Spirit and the Hierarchal Board to participate in the hierarchal plan and program, and who had elected so to be chosen. One of the symbolic 144,000 demonstrators and teachers for this spiritual program.

*elementals:* those intelligent entities supervising the elements which comprise manifested form in the Earth and astral planes, under the direction of the devas for those forms.

*El Morya Khan:* Chohan of First Ray. Prince of Neptune. El denotes Spirit and the Elder race. Morya is a code scrambling of Om Ray. Khan is a Sanskrit term meaning king. No Earth incarnation since Atlantis (despite claims by others), until present one as Mark Age or Charles Boyd Gentzel, a director of Mark-Age.

*Elohim:* one or more of the seven Elohim in the Godhead, heading the seven rays of life; creators of manifestation for Spirit.

*emotional body:* one of the seven bodies of man pertaining to Earth life. Does not in any way resemble the physical body, but has the connotation of a vehicle for expression.

*ESP:* elementary spiritual powers, the definition coined by Mark-Age in 1966 to supersede the limited and nonspiritual usual meaning as extrasensory perception.

*etheric:* the Christ realms. Interpenetrates the entire solar system, including the physical and astral realms.

*etheric body:* one of the seven bodies of man pertaining to Earth life. Known more commonly as the light body, the electric body, the resurrected body, the ascended body. Resembles the physical body, but not necessarily of the same appearance. This body can be used by the Christ Self for full expression of Christ talents and powers.

*fall of man:* sons of God becoming entrapped in the third or physical dimension of Earth 206,000,000 to 26,000,000 years ago.

*Father-Mother God:* indicates male-female or positive-negative principle and polarities of Spirit. Also, Father denotes action and ideation, while Mother symbolizes receptive principles.

*Father-Mother-Son:* the Holy Trinity wherein Father is originator of idea for manifestation, Mother (Holy Spirit or Holy Ghost) brings forth the idea into manifestation, Son is the manifestation. Son also denotes the Christ or the race of mankind, universally.

*forces, negative:* individuals, groups or forces not spiritually enlightened or oriented, but who think and act in antispiritual manners.

*fourth dimension:* in spiritual sense, the next phase of Earthman's evolution into Christ awareness and use of ESP, elementary spiritual powers. In physical sense, the next higher frequency vibration range into which Earth is being transmuted.

*free will:* man's divine heritage to make his own decisions. Pertains fully only to the Christ Self; and only in part and for a limited, although often lengthy, period to the mortal self or consciousness during the soul evolvement.

*frequency vibration:* a range of energy expressing as matter. Present Earth understanding and measurement, as in cycles per second, not applicable.

*Gabriel:* Archangel at head of the Fourth Ray.

*Garden of Eden:* biblical allegory; was not one particular locale on Earth. That period when man functioned in both fourth and third dimensions on Earth.

*Golden Age or Era:* the coming New Age or Aquarian Age, taking effect with the return of Sananda around the end of the twentieth century. It will be the age of greatest spiritual enlightenment in Earth's history.

*heaven:* an attitude and an atmosphere of man's expression, wherever he is. No such specific place, as believed by some religions; except to denote the etheric realms.

130

*hell:* an attitude and an atmosphere of man's expression, wherever he is. No such specific place, as believed by some religions.

*Hierarchal Board:* the spiritual governing body of this solar system. Headquarters is on Saturn.

*hierarchal plan and program:* the 26,000-year program ending by the year 2000 A.D. wherein the Hierarchal Board has been lifting man of Earth into Christ awareness preparatory to the manifestation of spiritual government on Earth and the return of Earth to the Federation of Planets of this solar system.

*Hierarchy, spiritual:* the spiritual government of the solar system, from the Hierarchal Board down through the individual planetary departments.

*human:* those of the race of man who became entrapped in the third dimension on Earth, forming a subrace.

*I Am:* the Christ or high Self of each person. Jehovah, in the Old Testament. Atman or Brahman.

*I Am that I Am:* identification of the Christ Self with God.

*incarnation:* one lifetime of a soul; not always referring to an experience on Earth only.

*Jehovah:* biblical term for Christ or I Am Self.

*Jesus of Nazareth:* last Earth incarnation of Sananda. Christ Jesus, rather than Jesus Christ; for Christ is not a name but is a level of spiritual attainment which all mankind will reach and which many already have attained.

*Jophiel:* Archangel at head of the Second Ray.

*karma:* that which befalls an individual because of prior thoughts and deeds, in this or former lifetimes. Can be good or bad, positive or negative.

*karma, law of:* otherwise known as law of cause and effect. What one sows, so shall he reap.

*Karmic Board:* that department of the spiritual Hierarchy of this solar system which reviews and passes on each individual's soul or akashic record. Assigns or permits incarnations, lessons, roles, missions for everyone in this solar system.

*karmic debt:* that which one owes payment for, due to action in this or prior lifetimes. Must be paid off at some time in a spiritually proper manner.

*Katoomi:* Hierarchal Board name for Lord or Archangel Michael. Titular head, with Lord Maitreya, of Hierarchal Board. Archangel at head of First Ray.

131

*kingdoms:* celestial, man, animal, vegetable, mineral, devic. Denotes a category of divine creation. Evolution is only within the same kingdom, never through the various kingdoms. Transmigration—incarnation of an entity in different kingdoms—is an invalid theory.

*Lemuria:* civilization dating from 26,000,000 to 10,000 years ago. Land area was from western U.S.A. out into Pacific Ocean. Final destruction was 10,000–13,000 years ago; allegory of Noah and the flood.

*light:* spiritual illumination; spiritual; etheric. Also, God as Light.

*light body:* fourth dimensional body of man; his etheric or Christ body; one of the seven bodies relating to Earth living; the resurrected or ascended body through which the Christ powers and talents can be demonstrated.

*light worker:* a spiritual worker in the hierarchal plan and program.

*logos:* a spiritual entity manifesting a stellar or a planetary body, such as a solar logos or a planetary logos.

*Lord:* God; laws of God; spiritual title for office holder in Hierarchy; designation given to one who has mastered all laws of a specified realm.

*Love In Action:* the New Age teaching of action with high Self, action with love; the Mark-Age theme and motto.

*Lucifer:* former archangel at head of the Third Ray; replaced by Chamuel after involvement in fall of man.

*Luciferian forces:* angelic forces who aided Lucifer in creating human form for man on Earth in the third dimension.

*MAIN:* Mark-Age Inform-Nations, the media outlet for Mark-Age.

*Maitreya:* counterpart of Lord Michael. Holds office of Christ for this solar system. Master teacher of Sananda. Name indicates function: mat-ray, or pattern for Christ expression. With Michael, is titular head of Hierarchal Board; Michael as power, Maitreya as love. He is of the race of man in the etheric realm.

*Mark Age:* designation of the latter-day period, when there are appearing signs of the times to demonstrate the ending of the old age. Also, designation for the Earth plane aspect of the hierarchal plan. Also, the spiritual name for El Morya in his present incarnation on Earth as leader of the light workers here during the Mark Age period and program, as executive director of Mark-Age unit.

*Mark-Age:* with the hyphen, designates the unit directed by Hierarchal Board members incarnated on Earth for the Mark Age pe-

132

riod and program, namely El Morya and Nada. One of many focal points on Earth for the Hierarchal Board. Coordination Unit #7 and initial focus for externalization of the Hierarchal Board on Earth in the latter days.

*Mark-Age Inform-Nations:* MAIN, the media outlet for Mark-Age.

*Mary the Mother:* mother of Sananda when he last incarnated on Earth, as Jesus of Nazareth. Twin soul of Sananda. Her Earth incarnations include those as Zolanda, a high priestess in Atlantis; and as King Solomon, son of David, mentioned in the Old Testament.

*mass educational program:* spiritual program to inform and to educate the world's population concerning the hierarchal plan and program of the Mark Age or latter-day period.

*master:* one who has mastered something. An ascended master is one who has achieved Christhood and has translated or has raised his or her physical body to the fourth dimension.

*materialization:* coupled with dematerialization. Mat and demat are a transmutation or translation from one frequency vibration to another, from one plane or realm to another. Translation of chemical, electronic and auric fields of an individual or an object.

*meditation:* spiritual contemplation to receive illumination, or to experience at-onement with Spirit or one's own Christ Self or another agent of Spirit, or to pray or to decree or to visualize desired results.

*mental body:* one of the seven bodies of man pertaining to Earth living. Does not look like a physical body.

*MetaCenter:* the headquarters of Mark-Age unit. First two were in Miami, Florida, beginning in 1960. Coined from *meta* for metaphysics and for Lady Master Meta, guide of light groups on Earth for the past 2500 years. A center for the practical study and application of metaphysics. Interdimensional headquarters for Hierarchal Board externalization on Earth. Mark-Age Meta-Center, Inc. is the legal vehicle for Mark-Age, filed in December 1961 and legally recognized March 27, 1962.

*Miami, Florida:* approximate site of spiritual capital and Temple of the Sun on Atlantis. One of the last spaceports on Atlantis to welcome man from other planets. Original location of Mark-Age unit, from 1960. Name spiritually significant: M-I-AM-I.

*Michael:* Archangel at head of the First Ray. Known as Katoomi on Hierarchal Board. With Maitreya, titular head of solar system government, or spiritual Hierarchy.

*mortal consciousness:* the awareness of a soul during Earth incarnation, prior to Christ consciousness.

*Nada:* Co-Chohan, with Sananda, of Seventh Ray. Member of Karmic Board of Hierarchal Board. Present Earth incarnation is as Yolanda of the Sun, or Pauline Sharpe, primary channel and a director of Mark-Age.

*negative polarity:* refers to the female principle in creation. The rest or passive nature, as complementing the positive or action polarity.

*New Age:* the incoming Golden Age or Aquarian Age. Actually began entry about 1960.

*New JerUSAlem:* the United States of America will become the spiritual pattern for implementing spiritual government on Earth in the coming Golden Age.

*Om; or Aum:* a designation for God. Means power.

*one hundred and forty-four thousand:* the elect, the demonstrators and the teachers of Christ powers during the Mark Age period and program. The number is literal, in that at least that number must so demonstrate to achieve the spiritual goal of lifting man into the fourth dimension, and symbolic, in that it does not preclude any number of additional ones from being included.

*physical body:* one of the seven bodies of man for living on Earth. Has been expressing in third dimension, but will be well into the fourth dimension by end of twentieth century. The vehicle for mortal expression of the soul on Earth. The physical on other planets of our solar system expresses as high as the eighth dimension.

*Piscean Age:* the period of approximately two thousand years now drawing to a close for Earth, to be followed by Aquarian Age. One of the zodiac signs designating a section of space through which the solar system travels around a central sun.

*plane:* a realm, a dimension, a level of expression.

*planes of action:* kingdoms on Earth. First, mineral: fundamental matter or form. Second, vegetable: intelligence to grow. Third, animal: self-realization of continuity; and love, feeling, desire. Fourth, man: self-consciousness of identity and potential of his powers; fourth dimensional frequency in third dimensional form, or animal body.

*positive polarity:* the male or action focus, as complementing the negative or female or passive polarity.

*prince:* a spiritual office and title, such as Sananda being Prince of Love and Peace as Chohan of Seventh Ray, and Prince of Earth as spiritual ruler of this planet.

134

*Raphael:* Archangel at head of the Fifth Ray.

*realm:* plane, dimension, a level of expression.

*reincarnation:* taking on another incarnation, on any plane or planet, during one's eternal life.

*Sananda:* Chohan of Seventh Ray. Prince or spiritual ruler of Earth. One of Council of Seven, highest ruling body of the solar system. Previous Earth incarnations: Christ Jesus of Nazareth, his last one; biblical Melchizedek, Elijah and Moses; Gautama Buddha; Socrates, Greek philosopher; leader of Abels, in allegorical story of Cain and Abel; leader of Noahs, in allegorical story of Noah and the ark. Presently located in etheric realm, from whence he directs entire operation for upliftment of man and his own second coming; headquarters is ship #10, in etheric orbit around Earth since about 1885.

*Second Coming:* refers to each coming into awareness of his or her own Christ Self, and the return of Sananda as Jesus of Nazareth to institute spiritual government on Earth by 2000 A.D.

*Self, high:* Christ Self, I Am presence, superconscious, oversoul, Atman, Jehovah. The spiritual Self of each individual. Differentiated, in writing, from mortal self by use of capital S in Self.

*self, mortal:* the spiritually unawakened consciousness of Earthman.

*seven in a circle:* symbol of Sananda and of Mark-Age unit. Signifies completeness, wholeness and the step before spiritual manifestation. Indicates the seven steps of creation, the seven rays of life, the seven major spiritual initiations.

*seven rays of life:* the seven major groupings of aspects of God; the seven flames. First: will and power (blue). Second: intelligence and wisdom (yellow). Third: personal love and feeling (pink). Fourth: crystallization (colorless, crystal-clear). Fifth: unity, integration, healing, balance (green). Sixth: transmutation, cleansing, purification (violet). Seventh: divine love, peace, rest (gold and white). As channeled numerous times by Yolanda.

*seven, unit #:* number of Mark-Age unit, as Coordination Unit #7 for the Hierarchal Board on Earth during the Mark Age period and program.

*sin, original:* man's mistaken belief that he can have an existence away from or be separated from Spirit.

*Son of God:* with capital S for Son, denotes the Christ body of all mankind, collectively. With small s for son, denotes an individual. All men are sons of God and eventually will come into that awareness, heritage, power and co-creativity with God.

*Son, only begotten:* refers to the entire Christ body, which includes all of mankind, and not just a single individual.

*soul:* the accumulation of an individual's experiences in his or her eternal living. A covering or a coat of protection, over which the individual spirit can and does rely for its manifestations.

*soul mate:* one with whom an individual has had close and favorable association in one or more lifetimes. Each person thus has had many soul mates, but does not incarnate with or come into contact with all of them during any one lifetime.

*soul, twin:* as an individual soul develops, it expresses in male and female embodiments. Eventually it will begin to gravitate toward either male or female for its expression in the Christ realms. While so developing, Spirit guides another soul toward the opposite polarity along the same path. Thus when one enters the Christ realm as a male polarity, there will be one of female polarity to complement and to supplement, with the same general background and abilities. Each person has a twin soul. But this term does not mean one soul was split, to gain experiences, and then eventually merges back into oneness. Twin souls are two separate individualities at all times.

*Source:* a term for God, sometimes called Divine Source.

*sphere:* planet, realm, plane, dimension, level of expression.

*Spirit:* God, Creative Energy, Creative Force, Divine Mind, Father-Mother God, Original Source.

*spirit:* the spiritual consciousness or Self of man.

*spiritual:* term preferred over *religious* when referring to spiritual matters, as there are specific dogma and connotation attached to *religious.*

*subconscious:* one of the three phases of mind. Denotes the soul or record-keeper phase, which also performs the automatic and maintenance functions of the physical body. The relay phase between the superconscious and conscious aspects of one's total consciousness.

*superconscious:* the highest of the three aspects of individual consciousness, consisting also of conscious and subconscious aspects. The Christ, I Am, real, high Self. The real individual, which projects into embodiment via having created a physical body for such incarnation.

*sword of truth:* denotes the use of God's word and law to eliminate error, and to guide and to protect spiritual persons.

*third dimension:* the frequency vibrational level in which Earth and all on it have been expressing physically for eons. Being transmuted into the fourth dimension, which was begun gradually by the mid-twentieth century for completion in the twenty-first century, but well into the process by the end of the twentieth. Does not refer to the three dimensions of length, width and height, but to a range of vibration.

*thought form:* an actual form beyond the third dimension, created by man's thoughts. Has substance in another plane and can take on limited powers and activities, based on the power man has instilled in it through his thoughts and beliefs.

*transition:* term denoting death of an individual on one plane so as to begin a new life on another plane. Also, general meaning of making a change.

*transmutation:* spiritually, refers to purifying one's moral consciousness and body so as to permit rising into fourth dimension, physically and as concerns Christ consciousness.

*Trinity, Holy:* Father-Mother-Son, Father-Holy Spirit-Son, Father-Holy Ghost-Son. The three aspects of God.

*twenty-six-million-year cycle:* a period of evolution for man in this solar system. The cycle since the final fall of man on Earth, during which the Elder race has been attempting to raise the human race that had become entrapped in the third dimension. Cycle to end 2000 A.D.

*twenty-six-thousand-year cycle:* the period of time, since the beginning of the fall of Atlantis, in which man of Earth has been given the last opportunity in this solar system for reevolution into the fourth dimension. The duration of a hierarchal plan and program to raise man from the third dimension into true status as sons of God. Cycle to end 2000 A.D.

*two-hundred-and-six-million-year cycle:* an evolutionary cycle for man involving graduation in and around the central sun from which we originated. The period during which man has experimented with life form on Earth in the third dimension. Cycle to end 2000 A.D.

*two-hundred-and-six-thousand-year cycle:* withdrawal of Elder race from on Earth, and decline of Lemuria. Cycle to end 2000 A.D.

*Uriel:* Archangel at head of the Seventh Ray.

*vehicle:* denotes the body for one's expression, such as physical body.

*veil, seventh:* final veil separating man from knowing his divine heritage and powers.

*vessel:* denotes a vehicle or a body for expression, as the physical body.

*vibrations:* the frequency range in which something is expressing; not in terms of cycles per second, or any present Earth understanding and terminology. Also, the radiations emitted by an individual, able to be received consciously by one spiritually sensitive to such emanations.


*world, end of:* denotes ending of third dimensional expression for Earth and all on it, physically, and entry into a higher level of frequency vibration, the fourth dimension. The end of the materially minded world of man so as to begin spiritual understanding and evolvement. Does not mean end of the Earth, but only entering a higher dimension.


*Yolanda of the Sun:* present Earth incarnation of Nada as Pauline Sharpe, a director of Mark-Age. Was her name at height of her Atlantean development, when a high priestess of the Sun Temple, located near what is now Miami, Florida. Also known as Yolanda of the Temple of Love on the etheric realm of Venus.


*Zadkiel:* Archangel at head of the Sixth Ray.